ALAN VAN ORMER

Book 3: The Rugged Desert Treasure in Paradise:
The Bolton Chronicles

Rugged Desert

By Alan Van Ormer

ISBN-13: 978-1-962168-58-8

Chapter 1

Wil Bolton's eyes popped open when his cell phone vibrated. "Hello?"

"Good morning, Wil. This is Sheriff Kanter."

"What can I do for you?"

"Three men are lost in the southern part of the Black Hills. A deputy sheriff is on his way to pick you up right now."

He yawned. "I'll be ready." Wil climbed out of bed, and had just slipped on his clothes when a horn blasted outside. Already? Wil combed his dark hair and noticed sleepy blue eyes in the mirror. The deputy had indeed arrived.

The two had known each other for a couple of years and Jerald was very interested in Wil's sister, Tessa, Wil had to grin because his sister told him she adored his green eyes, his properly shaved mustache, and short haircut.

Wil hurried out and climbed into the deputy's car. "What do we have, Jerald?"

"Three men lost in the Black Hills."

"Any details?"

"They were last seen in the Crooks Tower vicinity. One of the men was a banker in Newcastle, Wyoming."

Jerald Ankler glanced at Wil. "Can you find them?"

Wil shrugged. "That's a fair jaunt. Especially in this weather. What were they thinking? The weather is so unpredictable. How did they get out there without being seen?"

Jerald sighed. "Both good questions. You know as well as I do many people have a disregard for rules and think they can handle any type of weather. Now we have to head up there and find them." He handed Wil a satellite phone. "If something should happen to either of us, we'll each have a phone to contact the sheriff's office."

The two arrived at Crooks Tower an hour later. It had started to snow, but it wasn't too heavy. Wil searched the area for footprints. It would be difficult to find a solid pair in this weather.

Luck was on their side when soon three sets of footprints appeared in the snowy, and all three were men's.

Deputy Ankler flashed his light on them. "I'll call headquarters. He pressed a button. "We're heading to Crows Nest Peak."

"Ten-four."

They began the uphill hike. It was a good ten to fifteen miles to Crows Nest Peak, which was over seven thousand feet. The first few miles were slow going because of the deep snow. They'd traveled thirty minutes when they stopped to take a drink of water.

Wil looked to the north. The clouds looked ominous. "We're going to get socked by a blizzard, and we're going to be stuck in the storm."

Deputy Ankler sighed. "It doesn't surprise me one bit."

They continued up a path Wil remembered from past expeditions.

Ten minutes later the deputy stopped. He had come into some brush and found a piece of a torn piece of material. Deputy Ankler quickly called headquarters putting it on speakerphone. "We found something about an hour or so east of Crooks Tower. A piece of cloth from a coat or maybe even trousers."

"I'll pass it on. Deputy, you know a storm is coming in. Find shelter as soon as possible."

"Will do. Thanks."

They continued on along a grove of trees into a denser area for another hour, then stopped for a drink of water.

Wil surveyed the area when he did a double take. "Follow me." He hurried to what he thought he had seen, with the deputy right behind him. Several minutes later, he found something he didn't want to see. Big cat tracks. Another mountain lion was prowling the area. Wil searched the area but didn't see anything.

"What is it?" Jerald asked.

"Mountain lion prints."

He rolled his eyes. "That's just wonderful."

Wil called the forest service. "Amanda, let Hampton know we found a set of mountain lion prints."

"Okay. Will do. Wil, be careful."

He grinned. "You always seem to be worried about me."

She laughed. "Of course, I am. You're the only one I can joke with."

"Wow. And I thought it was because you thought I was good-looking."

Amanda Streeter chuckled at the other end. "There's that too, but so is Caleb."

Jerald laughed. "You two have a cool relationship, and that's good. How's the girl from Chicago?"

Wil sighed. "We won't talk about her."

Jerald scanned the area. "I want to have a relationship with your sister, but it's difficult because of the job I do."

Wil stopped and stared at Jerald. "Two things I'll tell you about my sister. Never lie to her, and never cheat on her."

Before he could respond, the deputy received a phone call from dispatch. "Jerald, three men robbed a bank in Newcastle, Wyoming, last night and are headed into the Black Hills."

"Do you believe these are the three men we're looking for?"

"Sheriff Kanter is right here."

He came on the line. "Yeah, we do believe it's the bank robbers, so be on the alert. The bank president's wife is here and told us her husband didn't come home last night. We didn't think much of it until we found out the man's bank was robbed last night."

"Do you know where they could have gone?"

"Her husband said Crows Nest Peak."

The deputy adjusted his hat. "We just left and are heading that way now. So you're telling me there could be criminals out here?"

Wil and the deputy stopped in their tracks. "Think we found them," the deputy said. "And they're all dead."

Sheriff Kanter blew out a breath "Send me photos of the three dead men."

Jerald snapped a few and sent them to the sheriff, who responded quickly. "The president of the bank is the middle one, but I'm not sure of the other two. Be careful! The killers could still be around."

"Ten-four."

Wil searched the area. "There aren't any tracks anywhere within a half-mile radius. The wind is starting to pick up, and it has been snowing, so they could have been covered."

When the wind blew them sideways, Wil eyed Jerald. "We have to reach the cabin over the hill there, or we will be stuck here."

"Lead the way."

Chapter 2

The next morning Wil's eyes popped open to the sound of voices. He reached over and gently shook the deputy who had fallen asleep on the floor by the fireplace. "Did you hear that?"

Jerald nodded. Wil jumped up and looked out the window. "Three men with rifles, and I don't know them. It looks like they're searching for someone."

Wil shut the curtains. "Out the back door and into the forest. We only have one chance to escape." They grabbed their rifles and their canteens before heading to the back door.

The deputy accidentally let the door slam shut. "Crap." They darted toward the forest when they heard voices behind them.

"Did you hear that?" one of them said.

"What are you talking about?" another asked.

"I heard something."

"Over there. Heading to the trees." a third man yelled.

A rifle shot sounded behind them as Wil and the deputy ran for their lives "Nailed one of them. Let's get them."

"Damn it, they got me in the shoulder," Jerald said.

Wil turned and saw the three men chasing them. "Down the hill. It's our only chance!" He grabbed Ankler and rolled down a hill with him. Once at the bottom, Wil jumped up and helped the deputy up, then they headed south.

Jerald grunted with every step holding onto his arm. "Why we going this way?"

"There is nothing that I know of south of here, but it's the only way we can go right now." He helped Jerald over the next hill, and they found cover before the three men could reach them. Wil and Jerald continued deeper into the Black Hills, then they stopped so Wil could tend to Ankler's wound. He did what he could to stop the bleeding. The deputy was fortunate the man was a little off with his shot.

Stopping to catch his breath, he glanced over his shoulder, noticing no one was following him. He sat Jerald down on a tree stump where the snow wasn't as heavy. That was one thing about the Black Hills — there could be a blizzard in one location, but two miles away, it could be clear. Which way to go? They were in the middle of nowhere.

Once they'd gotten their wind back, they trudged toward the west. Wil stopped. "Do you think we're close to Highway 85?"

Jerald shrugged. "Beats me."

They headed back north, and an hour later Wil saw a cabin. Hopefully, someone was there. The problem was it was winter, and the cabins were usually boarded up off-season.

Wil took his time with Jerald down the trail. When they climbed onto the porch, Wil was shocked to find it wasn't boarded up. He knocked on the door. When no one answered, he turned the door handle. It was unlocked. "Anyone here?"

No one answered. He pushed the door open and helped Jerald in. It appeared no one had lived here for a while, but it wasn't in too bad of shape. Will found an old wall phone, but critters had chewed through the cable. While the deputy nursed his arm, Wil surveyed the cabin. There was a bedroom with a bed with no sheets. At least it was sleepable. He went back out into the main room of the cabin.

A bathroom sat next to the bedroom. His hope was that there was something to help with Jerald's wound. He first had to get the bullet out. "Hey, Jerald, I found some bandages and cloth to wrap your wound." He walked into the kitchen area. There was still silverware there. He found a sharp knife, which looked older than he did. Wil would have to improvise. He tested the stove. Nothing. Why would there be?

He did the next best thing. Gathering old firewood sitting outside, he started a fire in a fire pit outside. After a bit, the fire was going strong. He took out his pocketknife and sterilized it with water from his canteen. After it was clean, he joined the deputy in the cabin. "This is gonna hurt a bit."

"That's okay. Just get it out." He winced as he removed his jacket.

"Try not to scream. We don't know where the three guys are." He handed Jerald a twig to bite on to keep from swallowing his tongue. With a gentle hand, he made a small incision with his knife in the deputy's shoulder. Then he felt around, stopping every time Jerald winced or whimpered. "You okay?"

Jerald nodded. "Do you see the bullet?"

"The dude was nice enough to shoot where I could reach it," Wil said. "Now count to five while I try to pull it out." He worried it out, then gently dabbed at the wound with gauze to stop the bleeding. After he figured it was okay, he wrapped it with the bandage he'd found and taped it with band aids.

When it was over, they both leaned back. Wil yawned. "You take the bed; I'll sleep on the floor in here."

After Jerald had retreated into the bedroom, Wil checked out the refrigerator knowing there would be nothing in there. He opened the cabinets. There were a few cans of pork and beans and fruit. He read the expiration dates. The fruit was good for another year.

Wil opened one can of peaches and reached in with his fork with his all-encompassing knife, after cleaning it in the snow. He hurried in to give the deputy some and then he ate some himself. The fruit tasted wonderful going down his throat. He grabbed his canteen of water and drank. When he'd finished his peaches, he crawled onto the couch and fell asleep immediately.

An hour or so later, Wil's eyes popped open. What was he doing sleeping when the deputy needed his attention? He jumped up and ran into the bedroom to check on him. Jerald seemed to have normal breathing. Wil placed his hand on his head and found there was a slight fever. Wil knew he needed to get him to a doctor as soon as possible.

He tried to push the door open to the cabin, but in the few hours since they'd last opened the door, snow had packed in front of it making it difficult to move the door open. He wriggled through and closed it to keep the warmth in. He checked around outside but couldn't find anything of use.

Wil headed back to the cabin to check on Jerald. When he walked in, he heard him moaning. He hurried back to the bedroom. "Are you okay?"

Jerald's face had lost some of its color, but he managed a weak smile. "I've felt better. Thanks for watching over me. I know your sister would be awfully ticked at you."

Wil laughed. "She would be, but she'd even be madder at you if something happened to me."

"You have a point."

Wil raked his hands through his hair. "The snow is starting to slow down, so I think we may be able to head toward Highway 85, and hopefully someone will find us. I searched around and haven't found anything of use."

"Let's move out." Jerald struggled to a sitting position and swung his legs over the side of the bed.

"First, we'll have to get something into your stomach; then we'll see if we can find some help. There are still a few peaches left."

Thirty minutes later the two began the walk toward Highway 85. They made it to the road. but the snow was pretty deep.

"It'll be a while before the plows get out," Jerald said. Wil nodded.

The two trudged ahead through the snow at a slow pace. Jerald had to stop several times. He was leaning against a tree when he peered at Wil who whittling a stick with his knife. "I'm slowing you down."

"We'll go as fast as you can go. Someone will show up, I promise you."

The two hiked for another hour, and both were starting to feel the effects of the tough walk through the snow and the freezing temperatures, finally making it to the highway. The highway was drifted shut and a snowplow may be the only vehicle that could get through.

Jerald dropped to his knees "I've about had it."

Wil helped him sit near a tree out of the wind. "I can't leave you by yourself because you'll freeze to death."

Jerald chuckled. "If we keep going, we'll both freeze to death."

"Did you hear that?" Wil's head popped up at a noise. He hurried to the roadway and saw the plow heading toward them. He jumped up and down waving his hands to make sure the plow driver saw him, but he kept coming. He slammed on his brakes just before hitting Wil.

The man jumped out of the plow. "Are you crazy?"

Wil wiped away some snow off his coat. "No, just happy to see you.

Chapter 3

Kelsey Lawrence stood in front of the mirror making sure everything looked good on her before she headed to the sheriff's office. Today she would report everything she knew to Lawrence County Sheriff Kanter, and her whole world would change in a moment. But it was time to tell everything she knew about the death of Lydia Boone two years earlier.

For the past ten months, she hadn't been honest with Wil, and during their last conversation, he had asked her to talk to the sheriff about what happened. It was hard for her to say she would, but if it could prove her love to him, it was worth it. The only reason she had held back saying anything was because of what her family would do to Wil if she testified against her family—something a Lawrence never did.

Kelsey didn't want to lose Wil, so she knew it was worth the sacrifice. She peered into the mirror thinking about the first time the two had met on Deadwood Street where he was counting cobblestones.

She smiled at how cute he had looked focused on the street. But at the same time, sadness lowered her smile. How she wished she hadn't persuaded him to join her father's treasure hunting outfit— something she wished she had never heard of. Since then, she'd lied to Wil about having a fiancé, spent time with a married guy in California, and lied about what happened to Lydia Boone, the girl he had loved. That final piece of information was the final straw for Wil. She hadn't seen him since.

Kelsey turned at the honking horn. She grabbed her jacket and joined Wil's sister, Tessa, outside of the cabin. She had come to pick her up and take her to the sheriff's office. "Good morning," Kelsey said, crawling in.

Tessa looked over at Kelsey. "Same to you. Are you ready?"

Kelsey sighed. "I thought I'd be a lot more nervous, but I need to do this because I don't want to lose your brother, and I have a feeling it's about to happen."

Tessa didn't say anything but drove to Deadwood, which was close to an hour away from Wil's cabin in Nemo.

Kelsey broke the silence. "I thought at first I'd be so afraid to spend time in jail, but the sheriff told me it would only be two years in prison and up to $250,000 in fines. I'd rather spend two years in jail than lose Wil."

Tessa glanced at her. "Let's just see what happens."

When the two arrived in front of the Lawrence County Sheriff's office, Kelsey laughed. "I wouldn't be surprised if my father had a hand in the building of this facility."

Tessa smiled. "This is one building your father has no part of."

Kelsey took a deep breath, turned, and squeezed Tessa's hands. "No matter what happens today or in the future, I want you to know that I am in love with your brother, and I always will be."

"He's in love with you also, Kelsey, but he has always had issues with honesty and trust because of our family's lack of it."

Kelsey swallowed. She hadn't done anything to deserve his trust. With that thought, Kelsey opened the car door, stepped out, and walked into the sheriff's office. "Sheriff Kanter, please."

The lady at the desk smiled. "I'll grab him for you."

Several minutes later the sheriff walked out. "Good morning, Kelsey, are you ready to do this?"

She sighed. "I don't know if I'm ready, but I have to do this."

The two walked toward the back into an interview room. The sheriff opened the door, and Kelsey stopped when she saw a tall man wearing wire-rimmed glasses and slicked-back hair. She turned to the sheriff. "Who is he?"

"It's okay. This is the county attorney who will be taking your statement."

The man smiled at her and asked her to take a seat across from him. She did as he asked. The sheriff sat five feet away from her but in her line of sight. The county attorney started. "You realize that if charges are filed, you could face prison time and a fine?"

Kelsey nodded. "I do."

"With that said, would you like to have an attorney present?"

Kelsey looked over at the sheriff. "No, we're

good."

After he copied down all the background information on Kelsey, he turned on the tape recorder and began the questioning. "Tell me about your relationship with Wil Bolton."

She turned to the sheriff. "Is that relevant?"

"Kelsey, he has to get all the information he can about what's happening."

She turned back to the county attorney. "I met Wil about ten months ago on Deadwood's Main Street. He was sitting on a bench, looking down at the cobblestones in the street, and said he was counting them. I think I may have fallen in love with him at that moment, and I still am in love with him. My father asked me to seduce Wil so he would join his treasure hunting outfit." She looked over at the sheriff. "Can I have a drink of water?"

After the sheriff stepped out of the room, Kelsey continued. "I couldn't do it, but I also lied about things such as having a fiancé, sleeping with a married guy, and the worst offense—knowing about what had happened to his girlfriend, Lydia Boone. The last item tore us apart, but then I'm sure you don't want to hear about our love life."

The county attorney looked directly into Kelsey's eyes. "How close were you and Wil?"

Kelsey's eyes widened. "Do you mean were we intimate? That's kind of personal, but yes, we were intimate. As for Lydia Boone, it started a couple of years back when I started dating Wil's brother, Cole. I didn't know who Wil was at the time, but I did find out from his brother that Wil had this dream about finding treasures, which intrigued my father, and that's what he assigned me to do."

The sheriff returned with a glass of water and set it in front of her.

She took a sip. "Thanks, Sheriff. Realize, sir, as a Lawrence you always work to help your family, and that was what I was doing. I found out about Lydia Boone, and when I heard that my father wanted to harm her, I called her and asked her not to drive in that car that night. She thought I was daffy and didn't listen, thus she died in the crash."

The county attorney asked another question. "How did you find out about the hit on Lydia?"

"I was in a meeting when Uncle Billy suggested it happen."

The county attorney looked confused. "Your uncle called the hit?"

She shook her head. "No sir, my father makes all of those decisions. The three of us were in the room, as was Cole, and then one of the servants brought in some wine that my father had ordered."

"Is the guy still alive?"

Kelsey took another sip. "He was fired a few days later, but as far as I know, he's still alive."

"Do you know how to get ahold of him?"

"I do." Kelsey provided the county attorney with the information.

After he finished writing down the notes, he turned back to Kelsey. "Your father actually did the work?"

"No sir, he called Eli Grafton who does work for father."

The county attorney shifted his notepad. "What kind of work?"

Kelsey took a deep breath. "He ends lives."

"I understand. You believe he was the one who took care of the accident?"

Kelsey nodded. "He was the one who did it. No question. My father has him on retainer to take care of those sorts of things. Grafton was the one who ended the lives of Cole and Del's buddy in Pactola Lake a year or more ago."

The county attorney looked over at Kelsey. "Why are you telling me all this stuff now? Why not two years ago?"

She peered into his eyes. "I told you earlier a Lawrence does not narc on a family member, but I want Wil in my life, so I had to do this. I understand what can happen to me, but like I told his sister, I'd rather spend time in jail than lose Wil's trust."

The county attorney turned to the sheriff. "Any other questions?"

Sheriff Kanter looked at a note he had written. "Kelsey, are you for sure that Grafton took care of the man in Pactola Lake?"

She nodded. "I found out that my father had been using my clothing-and-design company to ship illegal diamonds and drugs in and out of the country. Del and Cole were skimming off the top, and he found out. I was in the room when he ordered the hit to teach the two a lesson."

"Thanks." Kelsey stuck out her hands. "I'm ready."

The county attorney looked at her. "Ms. Lawrence, we have a lot more investigating to do on this, and we'll have a private investigator check on what's happening in Illinois."

Kelsey looked at the both of them. "I don't understand."

The county attorney's eyes bore into hers. "Ma'am, I have complete faith that you won't do anything stupid now, because if you did, I'd throw the book at you and your family."

~

Harrison Bradford tasted his glass of red wine and wrinkled his nose. It didn't taste the best, which was something unusual for a Boris Loe party since Loe had the best of everything. Harrison surveyed the party, spotting Kelsey Lawrence talking to Mr. Loe. He ambled over to them. "Mr. Loe, I see you've met the gorgeous Kelsey Lawrence."

Kelsey turned at his voice. "Oh my, Harrison, it's been so long." She reached over and the two embraced each other in a hug. "Where have you been?"

"In New York City."

Mr. Loe smiled. He's working with me on some major business projects involving the two companies, but he'll be here for a while."

Harrison's eyes remained on Kelsey. "I'm hoping we can see more of each other."

Kelsey shrugged. "Perhaps."

"I can understand your nonchalance. Maybe if you get to know me better—"

"We'll see."

~

Kelsey's eye caught a movement to her left, and her heart raced. Wil did show up, and she needed to talk to him.

Mr. Loe must have seen him also. "Wil Bolton, join us. I'd like you to meet someone."

Wil walked over to them. "Mr. Loe, it's good to see you again. Kelsey," he nodded.

"Hi, Wil," she whispered.

Mr. Loe turned to introduce him to Harrison Bradford. "Wil, Harrison'll be working with me over the next year or so."

"Nice to meet you, Mr. Bradford." Wil extended his hand looking at a man who was just a bit shorter than his six-one frame, had a tightly cropped haircut, and it seemed like he loved to show his pearly white teeth.

Harrison smiled. "I've heard about you and your escapades in the treasure-hunting world. It seems you get yourself in and out of trouble."

Wil grinned. "That's probably correct. What exactly do you do?"

"I work in public relations, and Mr. Loe has hired me to help market his treasures finds."

Wil eyed Boris. "I thought you had your compulsion under control."

Boris laughed. "I thought I did also, but Harrison has some unique marketing ideas that he's used with his own company that will be a big benefit to us."

Harrison peered over at Kelsey. "Could I have this dance?"

Kelsey sneaked a quick look over at Wil. No expression change. She turned back to Harrison. "I'd love to."

The two went out onto the floor. Harrison tried to pull her closer than she wished, so she pushed back a bit.

Harrison peered into her eyes. "You've grown into one beautiful woman."

Kelsey didn't change her expression. "Thank you, and I'd say you've become a handsome man."

Harrison smirked. "I have, haven't I?"

They both laughed. Kelsey looked up at his face. "You were conceited at thirteen, and you haven't changed at twenty-five."

Harrison grinned. "That's true, but have you changed?"

She sighed. "I'd like to think I have since we were teenagers."

The two danced for a few songs, and then walked over to Boris who was standing with his wife.

When Kelsey searched for Wil, Boris noticed. "Wil took off saying he had a big meeting tomorrow and wanted to be prepared."

Kelsey's eyes dropped. "Oh."

"Do you two know each other well?" Harrison asked.

Kelsey took a deep breath. "We did."

Chapter 4

Kelsey hurried to the pier at Lake Michigan. She and Wil had shared many conversations about moving forward with their lives on the pier. Most recently, they had a conversation that may have ended any relationship the two might have had—the conversation dealing with her involvement with Lydia. The bigger issue was the fact that Kelsey had been untruthful with Wil, and she regretted it.

When she didn't see him, she started to walk toward his hotel when a strong hand grabbed her from behind. Despite her resistance, the person dragged her toward Lake Michigan. She kicked and fought as hard as she could, but it was to no avail as a second man grabbed her, ripping her dress.

One of the guys threw her on the sand and pinned her down. The other one punched her in the face until blood spurted from her nose and lip. Then just like that, they lifted her up and threw her into Lake Michigan. When she tried to swim away, they held her head down. Darkness fell, and the sound of the waves sounded in her ears. So this was it. The end. God, where are you?

Through the fog, she noticed the men were gone, as she floated on top of the water with her head down.

Was she dead or had God given her a reprieve? She gathered all the strength she had remaining, pushed herself out of the water, crawled to the sand, and the last thing she saw was a man standing in the distance looking at her.

~

Back at the hotel, Wil ambled off the elevator on the third floor toward his room at the end of the hall. As he got closer to his room, he stopped. A figure huddled near the exit door. He inched forward. Was that—? He hurried over. "Kelsey, are you okay?"

She tried to look at him, but her head wobbled side to side.

He bent down next to her, smoothing wet straggled hair away from her face. "Who did this to you?"

Her voice was barely audible. "I don't know." Her eyes were swollen, her lip puffy and cracked. Blood streaked down her chin from a cut by her eye.

"We have to get you to a doctor."

"No, you have to go. Now." Her eyes remained closed.

"I'm not leaving you behind." Wil lifted her up and carried her into his room. He laid her gently down onto the bed and took a closer look at her. Her face was bloodied and black and blue, and it looked like her left arm was busted. And her dress was torn around the legs.

"Did he molest you?"

She shook her head. "Two men threw me in Lake Michigan after they beat me. They thought I had drowned, but I prayed. They took off just like that, and I climbed back out of the water. I didn't know where to go, so I came here. I'm sorry to put you in this predicament."

Wil peered deep into her eyes. "No, it's okay. We do need to get you to a doctor."

Kelsey wiped away tears. "You can't, Wil, at least not here."

Wil quickly packed his gear and set it by the door. "I'm going to get you out of here."

As he lifted her up, she wrapped her arms around his neck. He carried her down the back steps of the hotel to his rental car and placed her in the front seat. "I'll be right back and then we'll take you somewhere safe."

Kelsey touched his hand without opening her eyes. "Why are you doing this?"

"We'll talk later." Wil hurried back to his room and saw that the clock said three a.m. He rolled his gear down to the front desk.

"Leaving early, sir?"

"Yes, ma'am, I have to return for another meeting in Minneapolis."

"I understand," she said.

On his way out, he took his cell phone, pulled the chip out of it, smashed it, and threw it into the trash can. Wil climbed into the rental and saw that she was sleeping, so he headed northwest toward South Dakota—more immediately Wisconsin.

More than an hour later, he pulled into a Rockford, Illinois, truck stop. He peered over at Kelsey who was still sleeping. It was probably the best thing for her. He hurried in and grabbed some food and coffee along with some first-aid supplies. Amazingly, he found a public phone and called Boris.

"It's Wil. Please fly to South Dakota to my cabin in

a couple of days."

"Wil, what's happening?"

"I'll tell you. Be there on Monday."

When Wil climbed back in the car, Kelsey was still snoring lightly. Wil drove up into Wisconsin, past Janesville, and then Madison, hitting a rest area early in the morning. Once there, he gently shook Kelsey. Her eyes popped open. "You're okay. We're at a rest area. I need to put some ointment on your face, as well as check the rest of you. There is a family restroom. If you're okay, we'll go in there, and I'll look you over."

She nodded. Wil helped her out of the car. They were fortunate as, other than two truckers who were probably sleeping, his rental was the only vehicle there. He helped her into the restroom, closed the door, and locked it. "Here let me help you take your dress off."

When Kelsey struggled to take her dress off, Wil helped her slip it off her shoulders. He checked around her neck and shoulders and found a couple of abrasions and lacerations along the side. "Did someone try to knife you?"

She winced. "I don't think so, but I was so out of it they could have."

Wil checked her closely and applied some cream on the bruises. He helped her put her dress back on. "I'm going to lift your dress up once more and then your panties to check below. Are you okay with that?"

Tears traveled down her face, and her lip quivered. He wiped away tears. "Did they do something down there?"

"I'm not sure, but it hurts."

He lifted her dress and then her panties, checking her closely. "Good news, I don't see any abrasions down there, but you do have some cuts on your leg that I'll put some ointment on. Overall, you're looking pretty good, but you may have a broken rib that I'm going to wrap. Your arm is not broken, which I was afraid of."

She touched him. "I'm so sorry for all of this."

"Don't be. You didn't deserve this. I'll stay with you through this."

"You will?" Her eyes lit up.

"Yeah, the best thing would be to take you back to South Dakota with me."

She leaned her head back and sighed. "My prayers have been answered. You're taking me home."

Chapter 5

Wil and Kelsey spent the next several hours driving north through Wisconsin and then west along Interstate 90 in Minnesota. Kelsey had spent most of the morning sleeping, so Wil didn't make any stops along the way.

It was close to noon when they neared Jackson, Minnesota. She woke up and peered out the window. "How are you feeling?" Wil asked.

Kelsey groaned. "Like I was hit by a train. I'm so sore."

Wil quickly looked at her. "Are you hungry?"

"I'm famished. Where are we?"

"We're in Minnesota, maybe seven or eight hours away from Nemo. We're almost to Jackson. I saw signs for Burger King and Subway. Your preference?"

Kelsey grinned for the first time all night. "I can't remember the last time I had onion rings."

"Burger King it is." Fifteen minutes later after Wil parked in front of Burger King, Kelsey opened the door and smiled at Wil. "I really have to pee." She hurried as best she could into the restroom.

After Wil finished using the restroom, he grabbed the front page of the *Minneapolis Star Tribune*. Down at the bottom, an article's headline read: *Fourth Person Dead after Large Treasure Find*. He read on. Kelsey was listed as drowned in Lake Michigan. Dr. Richert and his wife were listed as killed in a car wreck, and Ivory Kitchen died after an overdose. "Wow," Wil said.

Kelsey tapped him on the shoulder. "What's wrong?"

He turned to her. "An article in the *Tribune* talks about you being the fourth person dead involving the treasures we found in Papua, New Guinea."

Kelsey grabbed the paper from him and quickly scanned the article. "Oh no, Ivory is dead? I knew he was into drugs, but it's hard to imagine he'd have an overdose. And that's sad about Dr. Richert and his wife dying in a car crash. But why am I listed as a member of this group?"

Wil shrugged. "Who knows?"

Her eyes widened as she looked at Wil. "Do you think you'll be next?"

Wil shrugged. "The other three deaths could have been a coincidence, but I have a hard time believing that your attack was a coincidence, since they attacked you and tried to drown you. They probably thought you were dead. Are you still hungry?"

"I am."

They ordered their meals and sat down in one of the booths next to a window. Kelsey poured ketchup on her Whopper. "I do like my ketchup," she said.

Wil rolled his eyes. "Obviously."

Kelsey smiled, then grimaced. "Ouch, that hurt."

An older couple stopped and stared at Kelsey, then glared at Wil. Once they left, Kelsey peered up at Wil. "They think you beat me up?"

Wil nodded. "Maybe we should go."

The two grabbed their food, slipped out the door, and climbed into the car. After filling the car with gas, they headed up Interstate 90. Wil stopped a few more times at rest areas. He pulled into Chamberlain's Arby's for dinner, which left three hours before reaching Nemo.

They ordered roast beef sandwich meals at the drive-through and were back on the road. After she ate, Kelsey fell back to sleep once more.

They reached Nemo around ten that evening, and Wil helped Kelsey into the cabin.

He placed her on the couch. "Do you need a drink or anything?"

"I just want to sleep." She tried to put on a smile. "Can I borrow one of your t-shirts to sleep in?"

"Sure. I'll get you one." He came back a moment later with one of the large t-shirts he'd purchased from New Guinea.

After she slipped it on, she looked down at it. "I'm just glad you made it back safely from Papua." She leaned against Wil. "Thank you for your help."

The next morning Wil sat on the porch drinking a cup of coffee. His mind raced about what had happened in Chicago. Just then his cell phone vibrated. Boris. "Hello?"

"What is going on?" Boris said without offering a greeting.

Wil looked toward the open area. "I'll tell you when you get out here."

"I'll be there tomorrow by noon."

Wil climbed off the porch and walked into the cabin to check on Kelsey. She was sleeping peacefully.

He reached down and wrapped the blanket around her body to keep her warm then went back out into the kitchen to start breakfast.

The sound of a car driving up to the cabin made him turn and look out the window. Sheriff Kanter stepped out of his car and met him on the porch.

He took off his hat. "Good morning, Wil. How are you this morning?"

"Doing well. What brings you out here?"

He unzipped his jacket. "Lot of stuff is happening, and we need your help."

Wil moved quickly. "Come on in. Would you like some coffee?"

The sheriff sighed. "That would be great."

The sheriff sat on a kitchen chair while Wil poured him a cup of coffee. He joined him at the table. "What's up?"

Sheriff Kanter tasted his coffee. "Cattle are being killed in and around the Black Hills, and the ranchers are becoming irate over it. We've had no luck finding out what's happening. Although you and Jerald found mountain lion tracks, the dead cattle don't fit what a mountain lion eats, so we're stumped."

Wil was confused. "What's happening with the cattle?"

The sheriff eyed Wil. "Maybe you should join me and check our latest find of cattle mutilation. It's like something back in the seventies and eighties when all the cattle were mutilated by who knows what. Some said aliens, while others thought it was some kind of cult sacrifice."

"Does the forest service have any ideas?"

The sheriff perked up. "There is a young lady —

Dr. Kimberly Wyatt, who works for the state. She has arrived and is starting to investigate. We figured you could help her solve this. It's scared many of the ranchers out there."

Wil stirred his coffee with a spoon. "Where do you want me to meet you?"

"The latest cattle mutilation was near Belle Fourche. Actually, it wasn't mutilation; the cow was shot."

Wil's eyes widened. "That's not in Lawrence County."

The sheriff nodded. "Right, but they have asked for our mutual aid. We do this at times when they need more resources."

Wil stood up. "I'll meet you over in a couple of hours."

"Thanks. I'll send you the coordinates."

Once the sheriff left, Wil turned at Kelsey's soft footsteps. "You heard that?"

Kelsey wiped sleep out of her eyes. "I did. You go. I'll be okay."

Wil looked concerned. "No, I'll take you to my sister's. She'll watch over you."

Kelsey touched his hands. "I can't do that, Wil. I don't want her to think you beat me up."

"She knows I wouldn't do that. You'll be okay."

"Please let me stay here?"

Wil looked at her pleading eyes. "Fine, but you're taking this cell phone, and if anything at all happens, you'll call the sheriff's department at the number right here."

Kelsey fumbled with her hair. "What about you?"

"The sheriff will be able to get a hold of me at all

times. Promise."

"I promise. Wil, I'll be fine." She blushed. "I'm glad many of my clothes are still here, but can I wear one of your shirts?"

Chapter 6

When Wil reached the ranch near Belle Fourche, there were already several state vehicles out there at the scene. The sheriff was standing with a tall woman when Wil walked over.

"Wil, this is Dr. Kimberly Wyatt. She'll explain to you what's happening."

She stuck out her hand. She had short, black hair and wore sunglasses. "Nice to meet you, Wil Bolton. Call me Kimberly. I've heard a lot about you and your exploits." When Wil blushed, she grinned. "I also have heard that you're very quiet and shy."

Wil changed the subject. "What's going on here? Why me?".

Kimberly explained, "Laney and Bailey Blue told me everything I need to know about you. That you've been good friends for a couple of years now. I've worked with Bailey in the past, and Laney and I have been good friends for a couple of years. Why don't you join me." She motioned toward two men huddled over a dead cow.

Once they reached the two men, Wil knelt down to get a better look.

"What do you think happened?" she asked.

Wil peered up at her. "I'm no expert by any means, but I'll give you my opinion. It's a coyote."

She peered at him. "You got that by looking at the site for a minute or two?"

Wil studied the area "I've seen several corpses around when I'm out searching for tracks. Not necessarily dead cattle, but I saw the tracks. Those are coyote tracks. I'm not saying the coyote actually killed it, but the coyote took a bite out of it." He stood up and studied the ground nearby. "Or in this case many coyotes." He pointed at multiple tracks crisscrossing each other.

"You're saying there's a possibility that a group of coyotes are causing this destruction?"

He zipped his coat down a bit. "I'm not positive. One thing for sure, there is blood here, which could mean the cow was shot first and then left for the coyotes."

"What are you saying?" the sheriff said, hearing the last comment.

"Sheriff, there are advocates for the preservation of wildlife, and that could include killing domestic animals in order to help the wild animals survive. I've run across things in the Black Hills I can't explain, such as coyote tracks in areas they've never frequented before or even bear tracks in the Badlands. Anything is possible."

The sheriff gazed at Wil and then at Kimberly. "What do you think, Dr. Wyatt?"

She lifted her shades up. "We have a lot of things to consider. Would you be willing to work with me on this investigation, Wil? The state would pay for your time, above what you make with the sheriff and national forest service."

"I'll do what I can to help."

Kimberly sighed. "Great, I'll contact you tomorrow, and we'll go over details once I put together an action plan."

"Is that all you need?"

She thought about it. "For right now. Thanks Wil. I look forward to working with you."

He looked at her. "Where are you staying?"

"Holiday Inn in Spearfish."

Wil pulled off his gloves. "Are you hungry?"

She did the same with her gloves. "Actually, I am," she said.

"How about we go to the Pizza Ranch for a bite to eat."

"I could do with a nice salad."

He opened the door of his truck for her, and they drove into the nearest town. Once inside the restaurant they could smell the pizza aroma, as well as see people carrying plate loads of chicken and mashed potatoes with gravy to their seats.

At the register, Wil purchased two buffets, then they found a place to sit to eat their dinner.

Kimberly observed the long line of people that circled the buffet. "This is sure busy."

"It always gets a lot of business. Everyone loves to gorge themselves with pizza or chicken."

Kimberly unbuttoned her coat. "I love their salads and their chicken. Pizza not so much."

After circling the salad and pizza offerings, they carried heaping plates back to the table and dug in.

Wil broke the silence. "You're not from South Dakota, are you?"

She grinned. "Does my southern twang give me away?"

He laughed. "A bit."

She grinned. "I'm actually from Owensville, Kentucky. I finished my studies at the University of Kentucky with a degree in fish and wildlife biology."

He massaged the back of his neck. "What brought you to South Dakota?

She took in a deep breath. "My fiancé."

He stiffened. "You're married or getting married?"

"Neither. We're through. My fiancé found a position as an attorney for the state's attorney's office. However, our engagement ended about a year ago when he had too many late nights, specifically with his paralegal."

"I'm sorry."

She relaxed. "Don't be. I'm so much better off. Right now, I'm focusing on my work. And you?"

He let out a breath. "Not the greatest with relationships either. I'm really close to Laney and thought maybe something was there, but she wound up with Bailey, whom she married. Before that, I dated Lydia Boone, who was killed in a car crash a couple of years ago."

"I'm so sorry."

"It took a while, but I'm getting better. I started dating a gal from Chicago and found out she knew about the death of Lydia, so needless to say, our relationship is still a work in progress."

Kimberly finished chewing her piece of chicken. "And I thought I had it rough."

Having said enough, Wil picked up his fork and dug into a slice of pizza, too covered to pick up in his hands. After finishing it off, he put down his fork. "How did you meet Laney and Bailey?"

Kimberly finished her drink. "At a conference a year or so ago in Pierre. Bailey and Laney were discussing Bailey's work in the Black Hills. Bailey also mentioned you and Caleb Streeter calling you guys 'the Chopper Crew,' or something like that."

"Yeah, we've been called that." Wil arrived back at the cabin around eleven. When he walked in, Kelsey was reading a book. She set it down and looked up at him.

"Are you okay?"

He gripped the side of the couch. "Yeah, I just grabbed a bite to eat with Dr. Wyatt."

Kelsey took a deep breath. "She must be educated. Is she pretty?"

He thought for a bit. "I guess she is. Even if she was pretty, nothing would happen, even if I wasn't with you."

She eyed him. "Wil, we aren't together. You just feel sorry for me because of what happened at Lake Michigan. You haven't touched me or held me or even made love with me. I understand why, and I'm doing everything I can to repair things, but you still don't want me." She stood up. "I'll always be in love with you, even if you don't."

Chapter 7

The next day, Wil joined Kimberly near Belle Fourche. The two followed coyote tracks toward the north into the Black Hills. When they had traveled for an hour, Wil finally called a halt.

Kimberly sat down on a rock and drank out of her canteen. "It seems we're on the right trail of the coyotes who made a meal out of that cow," Kimberly said. "What do you think?"

She scratched her nose. "I really don't know what to think at the moment. We may be on a wild goose chase, but we'll keep following the trail until the tracks run out, or something else happens."

The two continued for another hour when the trail ended at a creek. Wil scouted around for a bit but couldn't find any more prints. He returned to where Kimberly was writing notes on her phone. "Nothing. They just disappeared into thin air."

A gun blast sounded, making them take cover. "It's over there," Wil said, scrambling toward the sound.

She followed him at a distance. Suddenly he heard her call out. "Back here. There's a cow lying near a foothill. Careful. There are several coyotes who were enjoying the meal."

Wil whipped around and ran back to find her hiding behind a bush. He fired a shot into the air resulting in a coyote peering in his direction, then the group scampered out of the way. Wil hurried over to check out the dead animal. Kneeling down, he found the bullet hole, then eyeballed Kimberly. "I can't be positive, but it looks like the same caliber of rifle as the one we found earlier."

She continued to scan the area. "Nothing, Wil."

Wil pulled out his phone and called Amanda at the forest service.

"Hey Wil, did you find something?"

"Yeah, another dead cow. Get the sheriff's department out to these coordinates. Tell them it looks like the same caliber of bullet that killed this cow as the first one."

"Will do."

Wil turned to Kimberly. "A serial cattle killer?"

Despite the situation, she couldn't help but laugh. "You could call it that. There has to be a logical reason why this is happening."

Wil was stumped. "You would think, but right now the only thing I can come up with is someone's killing cattle to feed these coyotes, and that is total craziness because we both know that coyotes can take care of cattle on their own. If we have someone shooting cattle, it's opening up a whole new set of issues."

She sighed. "We both know feeding wild animals can alter their behavior and motivate them to approach humans for food, which can lead to more interactions between humans and wildlife." She went over to sit on a rock. "Any way, you look at it, this could be a large problem."

Wil's eyes snapped toward a movement near the side of the hill. "Did you see that over there?" he asked.

"What is it?"

"It looked like a person watching us. I'm going to check it out."

Kimberly grabbed his arm. "Wait until the sheriff's department gets here and have them check it out. The coyotes may come back."

"You're probably right." He took a seat on the same rock where Kimberly sat near the dead cow.

Kimberly stared at Wil. "What are you doing now to keep busy?"

"I'm in between jobs right now. I have a couple of interviews lined up for a fish and wildlife-service job in Idaho and Colorado. That's what I got my degree in from Frostburg University— environmental science with emphasis on fish and wildlife."

She surveyed the area. "I hear that Frostburg State is a wonderful school for that field."

He pushed back his hat off his head a bit. "It is. Right now, I travel around the world looking for treasures. That is interesting in itself."

They stood when a Wyoming sheriff's vehicle drove up. A deputy jumped out of his vehicle. "Another dead cow?" He issued a disgusted huff. "Anything else?"

Wil nodded. "Deputy, I thought I saw someone over there watching us. I had planned on taking a look to see what I could find."

The deputy eyed him. "You're Wil Bolton, correct?"

Wil nodded.

"Go ahead. Dr. Wyatt and I will do some checking

on the dead animal."

Wil started toward the hill which was maybe two-hundred yards away. Out of the corner of his eye, he saw a couple of the coyotes lying down keeping their eyes on everything that was happening. He kept going and reached a hill five minutes later. As he scoped the area, and he found some footprints, light footprints. Wil also noticed a chain of some type. He reached down, picked it up, and stuffed it into his pocket. Wil started following the footprints and lost them when he reached a small creek. He stopped and looked around, seeing an old farmhouse in the distance. There were no vehicles on the premises, so he'd let the deputy worry about it. When he returned to where the deputy and Dr. Wyatt, were another deputy and a member from the forest service had arrived.

The deputy peered up at him. "Anything?"

"I found some footprints, followed them to a creek bed, but then they disappeared. The person could have walked down the creek, but there was also an old farmhouse in the distance."

"We'll check it out," the deputy said. "Anything else?"

"Yeah." He dug his hand into his pocket and pulled out the chain. "I found this at the spot where the person was watching us." He handed it to the deputy who examined it. "I have a good idea who this belongs to. We'll take it from here. Thanks for your help, Wil. My partner will take the two of you back to your vehicles."

Once back at their vehicles, Kimberly turned to Wil. "How about joining me for dinner?"

"I'd love to, but no Pizza Ranch."

She took a breath. "I was thinking more of a nice

meal."

Wil's eyes widened. "Dressed in this?"

She giggled. "They have a restaurant at the hotel."

The two drove toward the hotel which was at least ten miles from where they were at. Once at the restaurant, the hostess found a seat for them and provided them menus.

Kimberly searched the restaurant. "I can smell the aroma of different foods and the photos on the walls make it appealing."

Wil nodded in agreement. "This is the first time I've been here but I've heard good things about it."

The two settled for steaks and cocktails. "Will you be okay to drive back?"

Wil nodded. "I won't drink all of it."

She grinned. "Then I shall. I need something tonight after the last couple of days."

Wil buried his hands in his hair. "Is this your first time in the field?"

She toyed with a lock of hair. "It is the first time I've been out for this length of time. Many of them are day-long trips just to talk to people, but this one is of significance to the state. The state has been getting numerous calls from ranchers concerned about the loss of their cattle. Some even bring up past mutilations that occurred in the 70s and 80s relating to alien abductions, and they fear it's happening again."

"I've read about that, but I don't know if there was ever a conclusion on what happened."

"I don't believe there was. Being out in the field is what I enjoy doing, and the boss has said I could do more of it. We may be working together more."

Wil's phone vibrated. He peered at the number.

"I'm sorry I have to take this."

"Please do."

Boris's voice. "Wil, we'll be having our first group of people in for interviews starting on Monday lasting a couple of days. Does it work for you?"

"It should." He got off the phone and returned to Kimberly. "That was my boss for the treasure-hunting group, and he wants me to fly to Chicago on Monday."

She gently touched Wil's hand. "How about a nightcap in my room?"

He took a deep breath. "Not a good idea. I'm in love with another gal."

She sighed. "The relationship you're working on?"

"That's the one."

She sighed. "She's a fortunate gal."

It was eight-thirty when Wil arrived back at the cabin. Where was Kelsey? A noise from the bedroom answered his question. He found her packing her clothes.

She peered up when he coughed at the door. "You're back early tonight."

"It looks like you're packing to move somewhere else."

She wiped a tear off her cheek. "I'm feeling much better, so it's time for me to fly back to Chicago."

He leaned against the wall. "You don't have to."

She rubbed her eyes. "I do because there is nothing for me here anymore. You've made your feelings toward me quite clear, and like I said earlier, I can't blame you. I'd hoped you would look at how hard I've been trying to be a better person because I do love you."

He sat down next to her. "I had dinner again with

Dr. Wyatt tonight, and would you believe she thought I would want to go up to her room with her and spend the night?"

Kelsey's eyes widened. "Why didn't you?"

He slipped his arm around Kelsey. "I couldn't because I'm in love with another gal, and I always will be."

She peered up into his eyes. "Did you think about going with her? I wouldn't blame you if you did."

He shook his head. "Not for one moment. You're the only gal I've ever thought about for the past year."

Tears brimmed her eyes. "You're the only guy I've thought about for the past year, also."

He stood up and took her bag to the closet.

Her eyes widened. "What are you doing?"

He leaned closer. "You said you were ready to move, so why don't you move back home here?"

She inched forward. "Are you sure?"

He lifted her into his arms. "Positive."

Chapter 8

The next day when Boris showed up at the cabin with a security guard, Wil let the two of them in.

Boris hurried over to Kelsey who was sitting on the couch. "Are you okay?"

She stood up. "I'm fine. It still hurts a bit."

Boris crossed his arms. "Any idea who would have done something like this?"

Wil jumped in. "That's why I called you here, Boris, because we need to talk."

Boris turned to the security guard. "He's good."

Kelsey looked over to the guy. "I'll bring you both a cup of coffee."

"That would be wonderful, ma'am," he said.

Kelsey brought them cups of coffee.

"Do you have any idea who attacked you?" Boris directed the question to Kelsey.

Wil answered for her. "My guess is Eli Grafton was the guy on the hill above Lake Michigan, and the two men were hoods of his, but we can't be sure. Would it be possible for you to have your private investigators check into what happened?"

Boris nodded. "That's what the investigators have concluded. How does what happened to Kelsey impact the Africa trip?"

Kelsey held up a hand. "It won't because I don't want Wil to stop everything he's doing because he has to watch over me."

Boris grinned. "That's why I brought one of my security guards. He'll be staying with you until Wil returns. I'll be checking in with you periodically in person and by phone. I hope that's okay, Wil?"

He peered over at Kelsey. "Thank you. I wouldn't want anything to happen to her." Kelsey squeezed his hand.

Boris ran his hands through his hair. "Okay, that's settled. Now I have brought some information on the different people you will be interviewing the day after tomorrow. I'll leave you some reading material, and we do have some real winners in this batch." He turned to Kelsey. "Don't let Wil make the same mistakes I did last time."

She smiled. "Wil knows what he's doing."

"Okay then, I'll get out of here and see you on Thursday."

"I'll be there."

Once Boris left, Kelsey turned to the security guard. "I'll set up a room for you, sir."

"Thank you, ma'am."

"Please call me Kelsey."

That night Wil and Kelsey sat outside with a blanket wrapped around them. The security guard had excused himself saying a new detective magazine was calling his name.

Kelsey peered up at Wil. "Don't worry about me while you're gone. I'll pull myself together, so I won't be a burden to you anymore."

"You've never been a burden."

~

Kelsey's voice came from the kitchen "Okay, guys, it's time to eat."

Wil and the security guard walked into the kitchen and smelled some kind of pasta. Kelsey had just pulled something out of the oven. "Just in time for chicken alfredo, my specialty, or I should say, one of my specialties."

"It smells good, and I'm hungry," the security guard said.

She straightened out her apron. "Clean up, and I'll dish it out."

Five minutes later Kelsey dished out three plates of pasta along with cheese sticks and glasses of lemonade. They dug in.

Wil's eyes were bright. "You continue to amaze me."

She grinned. "That's my hope."

Nothing was said for a few moments as the three continued eating. Kelsey broke the silence. "They're looking for a bartender at a local bar here in Nemo. I thought about applying for it. Do you know where the bar is?"

Wil wiped his mouth with a napkin. "Yeah, the Brandin' Iron about a mile down the trail."

Her eyes widened. "Can I walk to it from here?"

"Sure, but why would you do that?"

Kelsey rolled her eyes. "Wil, I don't have a vehicle to drive anywhere."

He leaned back in his chair. "Yeah, right. We'll have to take care of that."

She finished tasting her drink. "How? I have no

money. That's why I want to get a job. I can't continue to sponge off you forever."

Wil peered at Kelsey. "I have to fly to Chicago on Monday, and there are still plans for me to head off to Africa. I don't know if I will after what happened to you."

Kelsey smiled. "I'll be just fine. Don't stop what you do because of me."

He peered into her eyes. "Yeah, right."

~

On Monday, Wil arrived at Loe Enterprises to conduct the interviews. Boris provided him with an office that had a table and several chairs around it. On the walls were photos of some of the artifacts Treasure Paradise had found. The first few people who entered his office for the interviews were archaeologists.

Wil's first question was always the same. "What do you know about the Romans?"

Two of them had a general idea but the third — Dr. Abigail Brennan — provided him with a brief summary of how the Romans operated, and what led to their downfall.

When Wil asked her to elaborate, she counted out at least eight reasons including economic troubles, overreliance on slave labor, overexpansion, and military spending.

"Do you want me to go on?" she asked.

"Nope. What concerns you about going to Africa?"

"Most of what I hear about Africans' feelings toward Americans is positive. However, there are some Africans who believe we are arrogant and rely too much on money."

Wil found out she graduated top in her class two years earlier from Cornell University and had worked at the university as a professor. "What made you decide to apply for this?"

She thought for a bit. "Finding out more about their history, and what we can learn from African culture to help us today and into the future."

Wil interviewed several others for the positions of security guards and research assistants. He would have more interviews on Wednesday before giving his recommendations on Thursday to Mr. Loe.

Later that night, Wil sat in his hotel room and called Kelsey.

She answered after the fourth ring. "Sorry, Wil, I was doing something."

Wil yawned. "I can call back."

"No, I'm fine now. What's up?"

"Boris Loe is still trying to recruit me to go on this trip to Africa."

I thought you were going."

"I can't make up my mind. I really don't want to go to this party at Loe's tonight because he'll want some sort of answer and I'm not prepared to give it to him."

Kelsey sighed. "What's gotten into you, Wil? You enjoy this sort of thing. Don't pass up this opportunity. You may never get a chance again."

He didn't know how to answer. "Wil, don your fancy clothes and go enjoy yourself. I'll be thinking about you and praying that you're okay. Let me know what happens."

~

After changing into a decent pair of clothes, he

headed to the Loe residence arriving right at seven. He had been here several times before, and he still couldn't get over how big it was.

"Wil, you made it," Mrs. Loe said, greeting them as Wil entered. "I'm so glad. Boris had a good idea in having you handle the interviews. You are more knowledgeable about what happens in the field than he is. I know Boris wishes you would join them on the trip to Africa."

"Thank you for inviting me."

"The buffet is over there, and the drinks are on the other side of the buffet. Enjoy your evening."

Wil walked over to the buffet. Shrimp and lobster, but no hamburgers or hot dogs, which was what he really felt like eating. He turned at a tap on his shoulder.

"Wil Bolton, it's wonderful to see you, once more."

"Arnold Drexel, what brings you to Chicago?"

"The same as you I suppose. Colin and I are interested in what we can find in Africa." "This is my wife, Daisy."

They all greeted each other.

"What is happening with Archaeological Synopsis?" Wil asked.

Arnold took a sip of his wine. "The wait for this trip to Africa. It'll make or break our new business. Boris said you're not joining us, and that's disappointing."

Wil was confused. "I've never told him I wasn't going."

"That isn't what others have said. We've had benefactors drop out because you're not involved."

Wil rubbed his face. "I'm sorry to hear that."

Colin Jurgens joined the group, turned to Wil, and shook his hand. "I am glad you'll be handling the hiring of the next group to find the treasures and artifacts in Africa."

"Have they decided where they're going?" Wil asked.

Drexel took over. "The Romans did several expeditions in western Africa, mostly in modern day Eritrea and Ethiopia. They were looking for sources of gold and spices." He took a drink and continued. "In fact, the African Romans, as they were sometimes called, were the ancient populations of Roman North Africa who'd assimilated into the Roman-Empire culture. They existed from the Roman conquest until their language gradually faded out after the Arab conquest of Northern Africa around the eighth century."

Wil interrupted. "I read somewhere that they lived in the coastal cities of Tunisia, western Libya, eastern Algeria, and northern Morocco. Weren't they concentrated in coastal areas and large towns?"

"You're correct there. Some believe there are still some small factions of Roman culture who escaped into the desert areas after the Arabs came in. No one is sure."

Drexel nodded. "Some believe many Romans escaped to Lake Chad, which is located at the junction of Nigeria, Niger, Chad, and Cameroon in central and western Africa. It would be quite a discovery if it was true."

Jurgens cut in. "We do know that there were two Roman expeditions into that area, and there is a good chance we will find Roman treasures and artifacts.

We're talking about taking one of the exact trails the Romans took, hoping that something will show up for us. It's a gamble, but I have confidence that Wil will join us, and it'll all pan out, literally."

Chapter 9

Wil arrived back in Nemo in the afternoon of the next day. When he walked in, Kelsey was cleaning. He lifted her up and kissed her as she pointed behind her. Wil turned and saw the security guard.

"Don't mind me," he grinned.

"How was the trip?" she asked.

"I have it settled who's going with us. How was job hunting?"

She smiled. "I got the job and will start next week. Hopefully, you'll have time to come and join me?"

"I will."

They both turned when Wil's satellite phone went off. Amanda Streeter, who worked with the local fish and wildlife service, was on the line.

"I'll give him a call." After he got off the phone, he looked over at Kelsey. "I'm sorry, but I have to go. Someone needs a snowmobile ride."

She grinned. "You truly are an adventurer. I'll be just fine."

Wil called the number Amanda had given him. A younger guy answered on the second ring. "Hello, this is Wil Bolton. A gal who works at the forest service suggested I call you for a snowmobile tour."

"Thank you for calling. Could take us on a trip in an area called Trailshead Lodge?"

"I know exactly where it is. I can meet you up there when you're ready."

"We'll be there after lunch if that works for you. Ask for Cecil."

"I'll do that. See you around one-thirty." Wil packed his gear into his pickup and drove toward Trailshead Lodge. It was around one-fifteen when he pulled into the parking lot. With time to spare, he stopped in the lodge to talk to the owners he had known since he had been in the Black Hills. The lodge seemed to always have snowmobiles parked along the side during the winter and offered cabins, gas, and food. He turned when three men strolled in.

One man stuck out amongst the three, so Wil decided he was the leader. "You must be Wil Bolton? I'm Cecil, and I understand you're taking us on a snowmobile ride."

Wil eyed them suspiciously. "If you have your gear together, we'll take a ride." After the men left, Wil said goodbye to his friends and joined them outside. He noticed the three of them were busy loading their snowmobiles with more than what a snowmobile rider would normally use. He headed over to Cecil. "What are you loading onto your snowmobiles?"

He smiled. "We're from California, and we always like to be prepared. Most of it is winter gear in case we're stuck somewhere and need a tent to keep us warm, a heater, that kind of thing."

Wil nodded. What was going on here? "Let's ride."

Wil climbed on a snowmobile and led the group down a trail south of Trailshead. The group wanted to take a six-mile round-trip trek. It seemed the guys knew exactly where they were going, which made him wonder more about what was on the snowmobiles.

When they hit the three-mile mark, they took a break in the woods. Cecil asked Wil to show him around the area, so they spent thirty minutes hiking on an off-road path which at times had tough walking. They traveled up the trail surrounded by trees and rocky ledges. In fact, the two accompanying Cecil lost their footing and slid down to the beginning of the trail.

Cecil laughed when they struggled to climb up. "I think you've had enough of sliding down those blasted hills. Let's head back."

The two finally made it to the path. Wil eyed the men when they wouldn't make eye contact. "What exactly do you have on those snowmobiles?"

Cecil said, "I told you about the winter gear."

Wil shook his head. "Things don't add up. You knew exactly where you were going and when to stop. My guess is you used me to help you deliver drugs to someone in the area."

Cecil stopped. "Now why would you think something like that?"

"Just a gut feeling I have."

Cecil put his hands on his side. "I tell you what—when we get back, I'll have the boys open up the snowmobiles so you can see that we have only winter gear."

Wil laughed. "Do I look that stupid? Whatever you had on the snowmobiles is gone by now. That's why we took this little side trip."

Cecil grinned. "You should have been a detective with that inquisitive mind."

"Won't happen, but I do know that whatever you guys are doing, you'll get caught."

Cecil frowned but didn't say another word.

"Did you enjoy the hike?" One of the other guys said.

"I sure did," Cecil said. "Mr. Bolton here is suspicious of what we're doing. Open up the snowmobiles so we can show him the winter gear we've been hauling."

The two did as Cecil asked. "Are you satisfied?"

Wil didn't answer. "We should probably head back down the trail because a snowstorm is coming in."

"It's a good thing we have winter gear packed." Cecil grinned.

Wil returned the group to Trailshead Lodge around dinnertime.

"Why don't you join us for dinner?" Cecil asked.

"I'm sorry, but I have another commitment."

Cecil shelled out five-hundred dollars for the trip. "We appreciate what you've done for us today. If we're in the area, we'll know who to contact for a snowmobile trip."

"You do that," Wil said. He jumped into his truck and called the sheriff's office.

The deputy came on the phone.

"Jerald, you may want to check on three guys at Trailshead. The leader is named Cecil, and I have a good idea they're distributed drugs to a buyer or seller south of Trailshead."

"Any other information?" Deputy Ankler asked.

Wil gave him the exact coordinates of where he had stopped the snowmobilers. Then he drove back into Lead and grabbed dinner. He called Kelsey while he was eating. "Everything okay, Kelsey?"

"Yeah, it's been pretty quiet. In fact, it's always pretty quiet out here other than the wild animals yapping. How did your adventure go?"

"Everything worked out fine. I wanted to let you know I'll be driving to Craig, Colorado, in the morning for an interview and wanted to know if you wanted to ride along."

"I'd love to. I'll pack some things for the both of us. I know exactly what you need."

Chapter 10

The next morning Wil and Kelsey made their way to Craig, Colorado, for Wil's interview with the Colorado Department of Natural Resources about a wildlife manager job in the area.

While Wil had a meeting with the manager of the department in Craig, Kelsey said she would wander around the community to see the sights.

Wil and the manager sat down and talked a bit about the trip to Craig and other things before he started giving him details about the job.

"I'll start with the salary and benefits, then we'll go into the job itself." The manager shuffled through some papers. "Because of your experience with traveling around other countries and your work with wildlife in South Dakota, we'll start you at the high-end salary of $80,000 plus a slew of benefits that include medical and dental plans, contribution plans, flexible work schedule options and remote-work options, and career advancement throughout the state system." The manager sipped his coffee then looked up at Wil. "Let me explain a little bit about what I'm looking for. The position is based out of Craig and covers the northern part of Colorado's Area 6. We want you to provide recommendations and management plans for wildlife species and habitats by gathering and analyzing wildlife data." He looked at Wil. "Any questions so far?"

He thought for a bit. "No sir."

The manager leafed through some papers to find what he was looking for. "Collaboration is important in this job, especially with the staff, the public, external stakeholders, and land-management agencies."

"I can understand that."

"If there aren't any questions, let's take a ride."

For the rest of the day, Wil toured the area he would be responsible for, and later that night he joined Kelsey for dinner at a local restaurant.

"What did you think?" Kelsey asked.

"It is a beautiful area, but I don't think the job is for me. Plus, the manager isn't too keen about Treasure Paradise, even though he admitted it was the reason I scored the interview. He did say he would honor my commitment to Treasure Paradise, so that is a good thing."

Kelsey placed her hands on her chin and peered into his eyes. "It is, but you don't sound too sure about it."

He finished sipping his drink. "I'm not, but we'll see after the trip to Idaho in a couple of days."

"You're not going to Alaska?"

"No, that one's out. The manager texted me and said they had made an offer to a guy who was more versed in the area. The guy lives in that area of Alaska."

The next morning Wil and Kelsey headed west on Interstate 80 and connected with the U.S. Highway 191 north toward Salmon. It would be more than a nine-hour drive to Salmon.

Kelsey was reading some of the information that had been sent about the community. "Check this out the community only has three-thousand people, which is only slightly larger than Deadwood, and for sure the unincorporated community of Nemo, and it gets on average twenty-two inches of snow each year. Why couldn't we have gone south?"

Wil turned to her. "There is no guarantee I'll get this job, so we can look south if you wish."

She frowned. "This is your job, not mine. Remember, I'm just along for the ride."

Kelsey continued providing information. "They do have a lot of outdoor activities like rafting, fishing, and hiking through a wilderness area."

She closed her information packet and looked at Wil. "Tell me what an interdisciplinary fisheries biologist and wildlife biologist is?"

Wil thought for a moment. "A fisheries biologist focuses on aquatic areas, mainly dealing with the health of fish populations and the ecology that is affected by them or can affect them. I'd be examining individual species for trends, monitoring stocks for numbers, and assessing how they are impacted by the environment, just to name three jobs." He sipped on his water. "My job is to provide balance to the ecology and study the role of factors, creating environments beneficial to species survival, and working with conservation organizations. Working with wildlife I would basically do the same thing including working with government agencies, non-profit organizations, research institutions, and universities. The main objective is to develop strategies to manage and conserve wildlife populations and their habitats."

Kelsey's eyes widened. "Wow, you will have a lot to do. How will you be able to balance treasure hunting with all of that?"

"I don't know at this point. First, I have to find a job."

That night the two weary travelers made it to a hotel in Salmon. A tired Kelsey carried the bags upstairs while Wil checked in with the Salmon regional director. Once he finished, he went upstairs to join Kelsey. She was lying on the bed with her arms and legs spread out.

Wil sat down next to her. "You looked tired?"

She peered at him. "I'm exhausted. I'll probably fall asleep in five minutes. Are you hungry?"

He stood up. "Not really, but I'm going down to the hot tub and will grab something on my way back up. Do you want anything?"

Kelsey stretched. "Nope, like I said, I may be fast asleep when you come back up."

Once he changed into his suit, he headed down to the hot tub whirlpool and climbed in. A few moments later, a husband-and-wife team joined him.

"Is it nice?" the man asked.

"Perfect," Wil said.

The lady smiled as she lowered into the tub. "Exactly what we need after a week of traveling."

Wil moved over a bit in the hot tub. "Where are you heading?"

The man pushed some suds away from him. "We left New York City earlier this week and are heading to Portland where I have a new job. I'm really excited."

"Good for you. I'm actually here to interview for a job."

"You must work outdoors?"

Wil nodded. "Wildlife biologist or hopefully soon to be."

"Sounds like an interesting field," the gal said.

Wil nodded. "I got my degree in it, but haven't ever been able to use it, so hopefully it will happen this week."

"I wish you luck," the man said.

The three sat for another twenty minutes chatting before they climbed out and headed their separate ways. Wil stopped by the lobby café and grabbed a sub sandwich and water. He hurried upstairs and sure enough, Kelsey was flaked out on one side of the bed. Wil gently covered her up, and she didn't move. He finished his sandwich and drink and crashed on the other bed.

The next morning Wil glanced over at Kelsey who was fast asleep and didn't appear to have budged all night long. He lay there thinking about the interview coming up, excited about the chance to work in his chosen field.

When Kelsey finally stirred, she said, "Good morning. I was tired. Did you sleep well?"

"I did, and it seems like you did also."

She sat up quickly. "Are you nervous about today?"

He stretched. "No, I'll be good. What are you going to do?"

She took Wil's hand. "I'm going to the Sacajawea Center and Goodenow Designs for sure, then I'll see what happens after that."

"I'm not sure when the interview will be finished, but I'll text you when I get a chance."

"No worries. Every place I want to go is within walking distance of the hotel. It will do me good to walk after all the riding we've been doing over the past week."

Chapter 11

Kelsey's first stop was the Sacajawea Interpretive, Cultural, and Educational Center, which wasn't too far from the hotel. She had called earlier to sign up for a private tour because it was closed for the season except for private tours. Wil had provided her some money for the day.

She met the guide there at ten-thirty and spent the next hour on a tour of the place. He was just a bit taller than Kelsey's five-nine height and had a long beard that he braided. The man expounded on the exhibits that focused on Sacajawea, her role in the Lewis and Clark Expedition, and the Agaidika Shoshone-Bannock perspective.

Kelsey was enthralled with all the artifacts. The guide pointed out the beads and crafts, and other interpretive displays. After the tour, Kelsey made her way to the Salvage Grill for lunch. She wasn't that hungry so just grabbed a salad and drink. After she finished, she went to a jewelry store full of Native American stones, inlay and mammoth inlay, just to name a few things.

Kelsey sat outside on a bench. How would Wil's new job, if he got it, affect their relationship?

~

Wil had arrived at the Salmon region office at ten for his interview. The administrative assistant had provided him with a cup of coffee while he was waiting, but he only had to wait for five minutes.

"I'm sorry you had to wait," a short man with balding hair, glasses, and a noticeable limp, said. "I'm Quentin Kelley, and I'm excited about meeting you."

"Thank you," Wil said. "I've been looking forward to this since you contacted me to join you for an interview."

The two went into a conference room and sat down. Sitting in the middle of the table were donuts and a pitcher of water. "I love donuts," Kelley said, as he grabbed one. Wil did the same.

"Before we begin, I just wanted you to know the starting salary is $75,000 with full benefits including health care, dental, and many others. I wanted to get that out of the way so if you have any reservations, this interview can conclude quickly. Is the pay adequate?"

"It's fine," Wil said.

"Good, then let's talk. This area is home to the Salmon River, which happens to be one of the few undammed waterways left in America. The river and its forks are the only pathways into the Frank Church-River of No Return Wilderness area, which is the largest single federally designated wilderness area in the lower forty-eight states." He took a breath. "In addition, steelhead and salmon start and end their nine-hundred-mile journey to the Pacific Ocean in this region of Idaho."

"Interesting," Wil said.

"You can see how important this area is to this

region." He sipped some of his water. "In addition, the primary revenue comes from the sale of licenses, tags, and permits, federal taxes on hunting and fishing equipment, and mitigation payments from hydroelectric dam construction. Idaho Fish and Game does not receive any general funds from state tax dollars."

Wil listened silently, nibbling on his donut.

"Forty-seven percent or more than fifty-six million dollars of revenue comes from taxes and permits sold in Idaho Fish and Game. Fisheries has the largest budget, followed by wildlife, and as the information I sent you suggests, you'll be working with both of them."

Wil nodded. "That's a big reason why I applied for this job because I'll be able to work as an interdisciplinary fisheries biologist and wildlife biologist. It's important to me to have a balanced job and not just focus on one discipline over another."

Mr. Kelley appeared to be listening intently to Wil. After Wil finished, he spoke once more. "There are three challenges that this region has. One is chronic-wasting disease, which takes considerable staff time and pulls resources from other projects. It also impacts wildlife populations and sports activities."

"I have read that," Wil said. "Part of my job would be to detect, monitor, and manage the outbreaks, correct?" "Absolutely," Mr. Kelley said. "In addition, a second challenge is the presence of private land, and the impact it has on wildlife because there are landowners who are in opposition to enhancing and conserving wildlife habitat, as well as dealing with depredation issues when wildlife impacts operations."

He finished his donut and continued. "The third challenge is crowding and meeting public expectations.

Hunter congestion is a growing concern for hunters. We continue to do surveys to assess and inform management decisions, and we will seek methods to reduce crowding while maintaining the rights to access wildlife opportunities." He looked at Wil. "Are there any questions?"

"It's pretty straightforward," Wil said. "I understand that all the wildlife management plans are accessible to anyone on the Fish-and-Game website?"

"They sure are, and that's one of our goals—to improve public understanding of our goals."

Wil rubbed his chin. "I see you also have many programs: hunter education, general-trapper and wolf-trapper education, fishing education, and a master naturalist program. I would be working with these also?"

Mr. Kelley smiled. "You would. I'm impressed by your knowledge of what we offer. And that leads us to another discussion point. You are involved with a treasure-hunting group that travels around the world. We're very supportive of that, and if we hire you, we will want you to continue that."

"Why would you do that?" Wil asked.

"Recently, researchers in coordination with a local Native American tribe have found stone artifacts dating back about three-thousand years earlier than any other finds in the Americas. Fourteen projectile points have been found along Idaho's Salmon River. Some are delicately flaked, razor-sharp, and made of various stones. Your expertise in finding these items would be a boon for us and other systems throughout Idaho."

"When are you making a decision on who gets the job?"

Kelley sighed. "We'd like to hire as soon as possible, but this can be a long, drawn-out process; thus, we're hoping to make a decision by June."

"That is good for me because there are plans to go to Africa for a treasure hunt dealing with the Roman Empire."

"That sounds very interesting. Personally, I've talked to at least a dozen applicants, and you by far are at the top of my list, but I have to go through the rest of the interviews and other government safeguards before I make a final decision."

"Thank you for that vote of confidence."

"Let's take a ride and look at the region you'd be handling."

It was close to five when Wil finally arrived back at the hotel. Kelsey was stretched out on the bed reading a magazine when he walked in. She looked up and quickly closed her magazine. "Well, how did it go?"

"I have a good shot."

She jumped off the bed and hugged him. "I'm so excited. This is a beautiful place, and I have already found a house for us to live in. It's not as nice as the cabin that we live in now, but it'll work."

Chapter 12

It was mid-January when Wil and Kelsey arrived back in Nemo. Both were fast asleep as soon as they hit the bed. The next morning Wil's cell phone vibrated. He looked up to see that it was seven-thirty. Wil answered the cell phone and listened for a moment. "Sure, I'm on my way." He clicked off as Kelsey's eyes popped open.

Her eyes showed concern. "Is everything okay?"

He yawned. "It sounds like a couple of girls are missing near Newcastle, Wyoming, and law enforcement officials have asked me to help out."

"I have to work tonight, but I'll keep my cell phone near me. Please be careful." She reached up and kissed him. "I love you."

It took Wil more than an hour to reach Newcastle. Amanda provided him with contact information of Dr. Jerome Hanger, who was a well-known surgeon in Newcastle. Wil pulled into the address Amanda had given him. He stopped and glanced at the large house. It had to be more than three-thousand-square-feet nestled in a hilly area. He climbed out of his truck, walked up a small set of steps, and rang the doorbell.

An older lady answered, wiping away tears. By her

swollen eyes, it seemed she had been crying for a long time. "Are you Wil Bolton?"

"Yes, I am."

"Thank you for coming. We didn't know what to do. Come in. The whole family is here."

Wil followed the lady into a room that was larger than Wil's cabin. Sitting around were at least twenty to twenty-five men, women, and children holding each other.

A man jumped up off the couch and hurried over to him. "Thank you, Wil Bolton, I'm Dr. Jerome Hanger," he said, shaking his hand. "Please join me in my office, and I'll tell you what I know."

The two walked into a large room with a large oak table and a wall of books, mostly historical fiction novels.

The doctor smiled at him as Wil surveyed the shelves. "You would think I'd have lots of medical books. I love historical fiction, especially western historical fiction."

He turned back to Dr. Hanger. "Tell me a little about the girls who are missing."

"They aren't missing. They ran away." When Wil didn't say a word, he continued. "Franny is a sixteen-year-old hell-raiser from another family. Loves chasing boys. Our daughter, Heather, is the opposite, but they are the best of friends. Franny's boyfriend left her for another girl. That's the story we heard. Franny was distraught and took off, but Heather wouldn't let her go by herself."

"Do you have any idea where they may have gone?"

Dr. Hanger explained. "To the east there are some

higher elevations with a lake reservoir. They always go there to hang out for parties, etcetera. I'm not sure, but they may have gone that way. Otherwise, I don't know."

"They walked? Drove?"

"Unless they stole a vehicle, they would be hoofing it."

Wil followed with a question. "How long have they been gone?"

"Since last night. Didn't notice until this morning."

"Okay, I'll head toward the lake. Where is the sheriff's department looking?"

"They went that way also."

Wil sighed. "Dr. Hanger, if they're taking care of it, why did you call me?"

The doctor hesitated. "The two have run away twice before but always came back. I have a feeling they might not come back this time. Franny's parents want nothing to do with her. Heather has always been her friend, and the two are inseparable."

Wil started to walk out the door when Dr. Hanger's voice stopped him.

"One last thing, Wil. Please bring her back before the sheriff finds her."

He glanced over his shoulder at him. "I'll do my best." Wil climbed into his pickup and headed east, calling Kelsey as he drove. "Hey, I'm here in Newcastle and heading into a group of hills east of here. I have a funny feeling about all of this."

"What do you mean?"

"The fine doctor isn't telling me everything."

"Please be careful."

Wil drove past the lake the doctor was talking

about and continued as far as he could. He noticed the sheriff sitting in his car talking on his phone on the side of the road. Wil pulled over and waited for him to finish.

He came over to Wil. "Wil Bolton, what brings you out here?"

"Yes, sir." The two shook hands. "Dr. Hanger called me."

"Glad you're here. I have a feeling they're in this area of the county," he said. "There has been plenty of snow up here. Worse yet there are a couple of areas where people have been lost before. I'm thinking that's why the doctor called you."

He nodded. "The elevation isn't that high from what I remember."

"It isn't. But there is an area right on the Wyoming-South Dakota border that is hard to get to in the winter. This year there's a bit more snow than normal."

Wil cringed. "Nice to know."

The sheriff continued. "I'm sending Deputy Nick Parker with you. He knows that area best. Good luck. Here's a satellite phone that should keep us in contact." He handed it to him.

Deputy Parker, who stood six-four, walked over. "Howdy, Wil Bolton. Good to see you. I've been waiting for you."

"And you too," he said, shaking his hand.

"Call me Nick," the deputy said.

They began their trek up the trail of a hilly area. "This may be the highest part of the county close to four thousand feet. It's just outside of the Black Hills. Many believe it's part of the Black Hills."

"Do you know anything about these two girls?"

"Yeah. Franny has had a lot of problems over her lifetime. Her mom likes to sleep around with men, and her father is drunk and never around. And Heather? Well, her father is Dr. Hanger, so that causes problems of its own."

Wil looked confused. "What do you mean?"

"He's not an upstanding fine citizen that he portrays himself. The doc likes his women, and many say younger women, like sixteen or seventeen years of age. However, it's never been proven, although people are afraid of him."

"I don't understand."

The deputy scanned the area and said quietly. "Mafia connections."

Wil's eyes widened. Then he stopped and pointed. "Looks like a narrow trail that someone who doesn't want to be found would take."

The deputy squinted. "I don't see anything."

Wil walked toward the opening of the narrow trail and motioned him over.

"I'll be damned. I've never even known this was here," the deputy said.

Wil led the way, creeping along the trail through jagged rocks. At times they had to bend down or crawl or even slide on their belly.

"This is crazy," Deputy Parker said when they reached an opening which wasn't very large.

Wil sat on a rock by the opening and drank some water. He glanced up. "I'm so sick of blizzards."

"What are you talking about? It's just getting dark."

"No. We're going to get socked. We had better find

shelter." Wil stepped up his pace along the trail. They traveled another thirty minutes when they found an opening in the rocks. Wil slid through then stopped, the deputy bumping into him as he climbed through the opening. "You must be Heather and Franny."

Heather ran over to her. "Please help Franny. It's all my fault."

Wil peered over at Franny who had short, blond hair and was shaking. Heather had longer brown hair and the two were hidden in an area that didn't leave much room to maneuver and was cold.

"What happened?" Wil asked.

"She fell and broke her ankle. The bone is still sticking out, but I couldn't do anything about it. I'm sorry. But we had to get out of there. They would have killed us."

"Shut up, Heather," the deputy said.

Wil glanced at the deputy, immediately grabbing the deputy's right wrist to keep him from drawing his pistol. When he finally wrestled him to the ground, the deputy hit his head on a rock knocking him out.

Chapter 13

Wil grabbed some rope out of his backpack and tied the deputy's hands, then turned to Heather. "Are you okay?"

Her eyes were wide. "Just a little scared, but I'm okay. He's no deputy, and he would have killed all of us."

Wil made sure the deputy's hands were secure. "I drew that conclusion. Now we have to do something for your friend." Wil bent down and looked at the young girl who was still asleep. "It looks like her foot is broken or dislocated."
He gently lifted it, then snapped it back in place. The girl woke up screaming.

Heather quickly moved down next to her. "It's okay, Franny, Wil was setting your foot."

Wil scratched his head. "It's going to be swollen, and she'll have a hard time walking out of here, but I have an ace bandage in my backpack I'll use to wrap her foot." He rifled through his bag and found it.

Heather looked at him. "What else do you have in your backpack?"

Wil scratched his head. "Lots of items to use for situations just like this. There are protein bars in there, if you would like something to eat."

Heather's eyes were large. "I am hungry. Can I?"

"Go ahead and grab one for your friend." Wil finished wrapping the bandage, found a rock, and elevated her foot to help with circulation. "Okay, we'll wait until the snow slows down a bit, then we'll try to find a way out of here. We can't start a fire because the smoke will smother us." He rubbed his cold hands. "The best thing would be for the three of us to snuggle as close as we can to each other to gather warmth." He sat down near Franny and helped her move closer to him. Heather did the same thing on the other side, and within five minutes he could tell they were starting to warm up. The two girls were fast asleep within the next ten minutes.

Wil peered over at the so-called deputy. He'd be out for a bit. With that he fell asleep himself.

His eyes popped open when he heard a snicker.

The deputy grinned. "Oh my, look at this, Wil Bolton sleeping with two fifteen-year-old girls. What would the world think?"

Wil looked at him. "I hoped you would be sleeping longer."

He laughed. "Nope, you'll find out that I have a hard head, and you'll pay for what you did."

Wil ignored the comment. "Maybe you can tell me what this is all about."

He peered over at the girls. "That's simple. You won't get out of here alive. Since I haven't checked in at the appropriate time, they'll be looking for us, and they will have these coordinates. So, enjoy yourself with the two young things."

Wil frowned. "You didn't answer my question."

He stared at Wil. "The two girls saw something they weren't supposed to see, and Franny has a double whammy against her because she's pregnant with the other girl's father's child. Now how sick is that — a respected man sleeping with a fifteen-year-old. The guy should be castrated, but then I don't make the decisions now, do I?"

Wil lifted the two girls out of the way. "You, sir, will be here waiting for them, but the three of us will be long gone—back to the authorities across the border."

The guy laughed once more. "You won't get far. They'll track you down. That's what they do."

Wil didn't respond but shook Heather. Her eyes popped open. "We have to go."

Heather jumped up while Wil shook Franny gently to wake her up. When her eyes opened, Wil lifted her up into his arms. "This way, Heather."

Wil stared at the deputy. "Tell your friends to give it up." Before the man could respond, Wil slipped out of the cave entrance with Franny. Heather had already made her way out.

~

Kelsey looked at herself in the mirror to make sure she looked presentable for her first day on the job at the Brandin' Iron. She was afraid she would look too promiscuous in her outfit, but it covered all the important parts. She hadn't heard from Wil, but from past experiences she knew he would contact her when he could.

Chapter 14

There was still a light snow, but the wind had died down as Wil and Heather struggled with Franny down the hillside. For every few steps they had to take, they stopped to rest with Franny who gasped with every sharp move.

It took them an hour to reach the bottom of the hill where Wil found an area where the three could take a fifteen-minute break to catch their breath. While he waited, Wil called Caleb Streeter, a good friend who worked for the forest service.

"Where are you, Wil?"

"Somewhere east of Newcastle, and we need a lift."

"What happened?"

"Put simply, I found two girls. One has a busted-up foot and needs medical attention. Oh, by the way, we're being chased by people who want to kill us, needless to say, I can't trust anyone. Can you bring the chopper to these coordinates? We'll be there in an hour if everything goes right."

"And if not?"

Wil laughed. "Well, say hi to Amanda for me."

"We'll be there."

Once he was off the cell phone, he turned to Heather's voice. "Why can't they pick us up right here?"

"The spot were going is much easier to land and pick up."

"I understand."

"Good. Now we'll have to put a move on it because I thought I saw a four-wheel-drive pickup heading up the mountain toward where the deputy is."

Heather jumped up and helped Wil pull Franny up and slip her arms around their shoulders. They started the slow walk down a snowy trail toward South Dakota. Twenty minutes later they stopped and turned toward an approaching vehicle.

"They're coming," Heather gasped. "We'll never make it to the rendezvous."

Just like that a chopper flew over the top of them. Wil grinned. "Oh yes, we will. Let's hustle."
Wil lifted Franny over his shoulder allowing them to move quicker. They arrived at an open spot when the chopper started setting down.

Caleb jumped out and helped Wil carry Franny into the chopper just as a vehicle came flying down the road. Once Wil and Heather climbed in, Reese Winters, the pilot, lifted the chopper into the air.

"Where to?" he asked Wil.

"We need to transport her to Monument Hospital in Rapid City. She has a busted-up foot, there may be some internal injuries, and she's pregnant, so the internal injuries may have done something to her or the baby."

~

The owner of the Brandin' Iron gave Kelsey a

quick lesson on serving drinks and also talked to her about limits for people who enjoyed their drinks too much. He explained. "I try to keep track of how many drinks I'm serving to a single customer and also watch how they're acting, in order to make sure they enjoy their evening in a safe way."

"I understand," Kelsey said.

After another ten minutes of instruction, the boss turned the bar over to Kelsey. Her first customers were a couple.

"You're new here, young lady," the older man said.

Kelsey nodded. "Yes, sir, just started tonight."

The wife stared at her. "Aren't you a bit nervous? You sure don't look it. Have you done this before?"

Kelsey smiled. "No ma'am, this is my first time doing anything like this. What would you like?"

"Just a couple of beers," the man said.

Kelsey grabbed two beers for the couple, and they left to sit at a table. Over the next thirty minutes, the tables filled up, and she was busier than she thought it would be.

The boss joined her as she poured glasses of wine. "You're getting the hang of it awfully quick. That's good."

She put the wine bottle back. "Thanks, sir. I didn't know what to expect, but this isn't so bad."

The man laughed. "It can get hectic at times, and South Dakotans do love their alcohol, so we make a pretty hefty profit most nights of the week."

Kelsey finished wiping down the counter. "You're open all week long?"

The boss explained. "We're closed Sunday and Monday, but there are times when we do have a special occasion like a wedding party, or a local band will play, then it gets really busy. You wouldn't think it for a small, unincorporated town like Nemo, but it's like a hidden gem for people in the Black Hills and especially for those who camp out here during the summer." The man started to walk away but stopped and turned to Kelsey. "By the way my name is Nils."

Kelsey smiled. "Nice to meet you, Nils."

~

Wil and Caleb sat outside the emergency room waiting for the doctor to join them to tell them what was happening with the two girls.

"It's sad that any man would do that to a young girl," Caleb said.

"I don't understand other than there are a lot of people who believe they can get away with anything because of who they are."

They both checked their phones, and Caleb started playing a game on it, when Wil said, "Have you heard from Laney and Bailey?"

Caleb adjusted his legs. "Yes, Laney talks to Amanda a couple of times a week. It sounds like they're enjoying their time in California and have asked us to join them for a few days."

"Are you going to do it?"

"We're thinking about it."

The two glanced up when the doctor came out, a man with shaggy eyebrows that matched his mustache. He sat down across from them. "What a situation. Heather will be just fine while the other girl, Frances, has plenty of complications that include a broken foot and the loss of her baby."

Wil sighed. "That's so sad. Will Franny be okay?"

"It's too soon to tell. Do either of you know if she has any relatives?"

They both shook their heads.

"I'll have the administration see what they can find out. It'll be some time before Franny will be able to leave, but Heather should be able to go home tomorrow. I'm sure it's the same situation with her — no family."

"Her dad is Dr. Jerome Hanger."

"Oh, thought I recognized the name. I know Dr. Hanger. Why isn't he here?"

Wil didn't respond, evading his gaze.

A perplexed doctor asked, "Is there something going on I should know about?"

"It's best if you talk to the sheriff's department," Wil said.

It was three in the morning when Wil arrived back in his cabin. He opened the door, and Kelsey was fast asleep on the couch wrapped in a blanket. He sat down beside her and shook her gently. "Wouldn't you feel more comfortable in bed?"

She opened her eyes, quickly moved over to him, and held him. "I was so worried about you when I didn't hear anything from you and thought something had happened." She smacked him in his arms. "Couldn't you at least have called me to tell me everything was okay?"

"Calm down," Wil said.

She eyed him. "Don't tell me to calm down when I don't know what's happening with you."

"I promise I'll tell you next time."

Kelsey let out a sigh of relief. "Thank you. Now I can go to bed." When he shook his head, she glanced at him. "What?" she asked. "All I needed to know was that you're okay, then I'd be okay. Good night."

The next morning Wil walked out to the smell of bacon. Kelsey turned to him. "Do you have all your bags packed for your trip to Africa?" When he stopped in his tracks, she grinned. "Don't you remember you told me you had to catch a flight to Chicago this morning?"

"Yeah, but that was a couple of weeks ago."

"I remember important details. Let's eat some breakfast."

While they were eating, Wil mentioned the pickup. "Why don't you drive me to the airport, so you'll have the truck if you need it?"

"Are you sure about that?"

"We're good."

"Deal."

After breakfast the two drove toward Rapid City Airport. Wil parked in front so he could unload his gear. Kelsey walked around from the passenger side to join him on the driver's side. She wrapped her arms around his neck. "Please be careful." She kissed him passionately, turned, and hopped into the pickup. He stared at her as she drove away. He could get used to this.

Chapter 15

The group was sitting on the plane ready for the ten-hour flight to Tunisia. Tunis was the capital and largest city in the country and often referred to as 'Grand Tunis.' The city had more than 2.7 million people and was considered the third largest city in the region after Casablanca and Algiers, and the eleventh largest in the Arab world.

Wil surveyed the team, noticing Dr. Abigail Brennan talking with the two research assistants, Delilah and Mitch, both who had started dating each other after their last trip together to Yosemite National Park, where Mitch had busted his leg. Boris Loe had brought them both to Chicago to work in the gallery.

"Congratulations on your marriage," Wil said when he joined them.

"Thanks Wil," Mitch said. "We didn't want to miss this."

Over in another corner of the plane, Vivian Tusk was checking all of her medical gear. She was the team's nurse and had been a big help in helping Tito, the Japanese guard in a Papua, New Guinea cave, survive a gunshot wound from Xavier Holloman, an employee of Kelsey's father, Hank Lawrence. Wil expected to see Holloman somewhere during the trip.

Also involved was Zachary Bill, a historian from the University of Chicago, who happened to be a good friend of Loe. He was talking to the group's security head, Abraham Donald. The guy was a former Army Ranger who had gotten out of the service just two years ago.

The group was waiting to meet their guide, Ahman Lazaar. He was gathering the necessary gear and transportation to follow the route the Romans had taken between the first century BC and the fourth century AD.

Once the plane took off from O'Hare Airport, Wil gathered them all in a conference room to have Zachary provide a briefing on the history relevant to the trip. Everyone gathered around as Mitch helped Zachary set up his slide show.

Zachary sipped on his water and smiled at everyone. "I'm excited about what we're about to do in the next month or so. We may be involved in one of the greatest finds of our time. Two Roman expeditions were carried out in the first century AD to reach Lake Chad, which was a huge lake at the time." He took another drink. "Septimius Flaccus and Julius Maternus reached the 'lake of hippopotamus,' which was what Ptolemy called Lake Chad. The Romans were able to leave a small garrison on the lake." He looked around at the other. "There is hope that we can find some remains of what the Romans left there. If we're successful, it'll be a fantastic find."

Zachary flipped another slide. "Now, I'll talk a little bit about Lake Chad, which is a freshwater lake located at the junction of Nigeria, Niger, Chad, and

Cameroon in central and western Africa. As you can imagine, it is an important wetland ecosystem in the region. Climate change and water diversion has reduced the lake since the mid-1970s. In the nineteenth century, the area of the lake was more than twenty-eight-thousand square kilometers. Today it fluctuates between two-thousand and five-thousand square kilometers, which shows there has been a drastic change."

Zachary showed a map of the Sahara-Desert ecoregion. "As you can see, this area is more than 4.6 million square kilometers, which includes the areas we'll be searching — Chad, Libya, and Niger. Vegetation is rare, rainfall is minimal and sporadic, and the ecoregion consists mostly of sand dunes, stone plateaus, dry valleys, gravel plains, and salt flats."

Vivian, with her red hair and wire-rimmed glasses, stepped up to the front. "Good morning, as Zachary said, this is going to be an exciting venture, but realize deserts are dangerous, and the land varies from area to area. The Sahara Desert spans over 3.6 million square miles, which is almost one-third of the continent." She guzzled some of her water. "I've made sure that we have essentials on this trip that include long, comfortable pants for walking and leg protection when riding camels, a light jacket, hat, and a scarf to wrap around your head and face for protection from blowing sand and sun." She continued. "We've brought plenty of sunscreen, and I made sure your list consists of sneakers, hiking boots, and hiking sandals. We also have several cameras, with batteries and a brush to clear sand off the camera lens."

Dr. Brennan was the last one to speak. "Like

Zachary and Vivian said, we could be making history on this trip. For me, this is the first time I'll be able to work with ground-penetrating radar or GPR which helps search for ancient cities and settlements hidden underneath the sand." She popped up a slide that showed a GPR machine. "It's a non-destructive, geophysical method using radar pulses to image the subsurface. What's cool about it—it emits high-frequency, electromagnetic waves into the ground, which reflect off rocks, soil, and buried structures." She continued. "While we're searching for Roman artifacts, it's also important to realize that Saharan rock art is an important piece of archaeology because it dates back twelve-thousand years and offers a glimpse of ancient African societies. There are all kinds of possibilities out there."

Wil stood up front and peered at the group. "It seems like I always get to finish everything off by talking about the dangers associated with any trip. There are plenty dealing with the Sahara Desert. While it's a treasure in this region of the world, it's also dangerous."

A few of the group offered a weak chuckle.

He slipped on the first slide. "We'll start with the extreme temperatures. During the day it can reach 120 degrees, and at night it can drop below freezing, which as everyone knows, leads to heatstroke in the day and hypothermia at night."

Wil flipped the next slide. "Dehydration due to a lack of water can be a significant danger. That's why we're making sure we have plenty of water for this trip—as much as three months' worth of water. We will come across water sources in the Sahara, but it's important to remember to filter the water before drinking. It includes boiling water for at least five minutes to kill any bacteria. This also means that you have to boil the water before you brush your teeth."

He turned to the group as the next slide popped up. "Vivian will monitor your hydration levels for signs of dry mouth, headache, fatigue, or dizziness. I expect each one of you to heed her words because I know firsthand that she can save a life."

Their eyes widened at the next slide.

"As you can tell, these people can see nothing during this sandstorm. and these powerful storms can occur without warning which makes it difficult to seek shelter. If this happens, cover your mouth and nose with a cloth or mask to avoid inhaling sand particles."

They all gasped at the next slide showing a scorpion.

"It seems like everywhere we go exploring, we run into some kind of venomous creature. There are sand vipers, venomous snakes that can grow up to eighty-five centimeters, or thirty-four inches; a silver ant that is only active ten minutes a day but the little guy doesn't waste time; and the most poisonous scorpion in the world—the deathstalker scorpion produces a lethal cocktail of neurotoxins, and its bite can cause excruciating pain and even death."

He flipped the next slide. "Yes, there are even desert crocodiles in the Sahara. They inhabit isolated oases and wadis." He turned off the LCD machine. "To finish it off, the main thing is for all of us to use common sense and listen to what the experts have to say about the environment over there. That's why they're here."

Chapter 16

"We're in Tunis, and it's already 100 degrees, and it's only April." Wil grumbled.

Kelsey laughed. "You realize it's cold and snowy here."

"Yeah, that's probably true. How are you doing?"

"I'm feeling much better, and the job is going fine. I really enjoy it because the people are so kind to me. Many have tried to pick me up, but that ends quickly when they find out I'm with you. I am still with you, aren't I?"

"You'll always be the one."

Kelsey sighed. "That's so good to hear. Please be safe in Africa and find all the treasures you can. I'll be thinking of you, but then I'm always doing that."

As soon as he closed his cell phone, there was a knock on the door. He opened it to see Vivian standing there with Dr. Brennan.

Vivian spoke up. "We're going down to get a drink and thought you may want to join us."

"Give me a moment, and I'll be right with you."

The trio took the elevator down to the dining room where they also served drinks. Along with the others, Wil ordered a drink and sat back enjoying the peacefulness of the lounge. No one else was in the room while they were there.

Dr. Brennan grinned at Wil. "Loved your speech. You were right—you got to deliver all the bad news to everyone, but you realize that usually nothing dangerous happens."

Wil tasted his drink and then answered. "Yep, but there is always that one time, like in Papua, New Guinea when one of the guys with us was shot. If Vivian wasn't there, who knows what would have happened."

Vivian sipped her drink. "You would have gotten us out of the situation. I have no doubts about that."

Wil turned his attention to Dr. Brennan. "Thanks. What do you really hope we'll get out of this, Dr. Brennan?"

She had just finished her drink. "First off, call me Abbie. That's my name. In response to your question, I'm not sure, but my gut tells me we won't find those coins."

"Why not?" Vivian asked.

Abbie sipped her wine. "Because I just can't imagine there would be that many coins in stock after Caesar died. I'm not an expert of the Roman Empire by any means, but throughout history once someone is deposed of, killed, or whatever, their successor tries to get rid of everything associated with that person as soon as possible."

"Except," Wil said, "that Caesar was somewhat of an icon for Rome."

"That's true," Abbie said. "We'll just have to see."

Wil stood up. "Well, it's been fun. Tomorrow we're going to see our first Roman architecture feature

— the amphitheater of El Djem."

"That will be awesome," Abbie said.

The next morning the crew was waiting down in the lobby of the hotel when a bald-headed man with wire-rimmed glasses stepped in and looked around. Wil hurried over to him. "Ahman Lazaar?"

"Yes, sir. You must be Wil Bolton."

Wil proffered his hand. "I am."

"Wonderful, we have a couple of vehicles waiting outside for our trip to El Djem. A historian will be waiting there to give us a tour."

The group climbed into three vehicles. Wil joined Ahman, Abbie, and Vivian in one vehicle while the others filled into the other two.

"It's a two-hour drive to El Djem," Ahman said. "You may know this, but the amphitheater could seat thirty-five thousand spectators with only the Colosseum in Rome and the ruined theater of Capua being larger. As you can guess, it was mainly used for gladiator shows and chariot races. The ruins were declared a World Heritage site in 1979."

It was close to eleven when the group pulled into the amphitheater area. Waiting for them was a gal with gray, long hair down past shoulders, wearing a pair of jeans and jacket. "I'm Scarlett Boyer from England and have been studying these ruins for a couple of years now. They are magnificent. Please let me show you." They strolled around the colosseum starting with the southern side. "This is the best-preserved part of the feature," Scarlett said, pointing up to an area where there was bench seating. "I see many people sit up there and imagine them cheering for the gladiators and the beasts."

Many climbed the stairs to the seating area and sat down to look around. Mitch and Delilah sat with Wil.

Mitch shook his head. "It's hard to imagine how barbaric the Romans were in that period of time."

Wil shifted in his seat to talk to Mitch. "Yeah, but those who rule have been barbaric throughout our history. It's one way they control others, and the Romans were a powerful empire for many centuries."

It was almost noon when the group headed down to an area in an underground passageway where there was lunch for everyone. There was a variety of different foods including *Brik*, a pastry made with a cooked egg; a mini sandwich called *fricasse*, filled with tuna, boiled egg, and potato; and pita sandwiches.

"This is very nice," Vivian said to Scarlett. "What is this? It looks like a doughnut."

Scarlett smiled. "It is. Or what the natives call, *Bambalouni*." An hour later Scarlett led the group down a dozen stairs into an underground passage that was made of rock walls. Wil touched the walls to see what they were made of.

Scarlet must have noticed. "After all these years, it is still solid."

Vivian stopped right in front of Wil, who almost ran into her. "Wil, what do you think that shining thing is in that gap down there?" She pointed at a lower level of the wall.

Wil and Scarlett walked over to where she pointed. He grabbed a stick that he found lying on the ground and poked it into the gap. What looked like a ring came out on the stick.

"Wow, is that an ancient Roman ring?" Abbie hurried over to the trio.

"It sure looks like it," Scarlett said.

Wil handed it over to her. "It appears to be an ancient Roman garnet—inlaid with gold. It most likely comes from the first century AD. What a find!"

Scarlett peered at Wil. "And it's all yours."

"How can that be?" Abbie asked.

Scarlett looked at her. "Many of these items are sold in antique shops around the country. I know Mr. Loe would enjoy having this ring for his collection."

"Have you seen his collection?" Mitch asked.

"Several times, and that's why I agreed to help with this project."

The group spent the day strolling around the theater, and by nightfall they headed back to Tunis.

After they pulled into their hotel and walked inside, Ahman and Wil grabbed a bite to eat in the restaurant while many of the others went to the swimming-pool area to cool off.

Ahman peered at his meal. "The vehicles will be ready to go tomorrow. One problem is you won't be able to go to Lake Chad as you wished. The surrounding forests are a Boko Haram hideout, and it's unlikely you would be able to obtain access to the lake."

Wil pulled out a map of western Africa. "How about this route through Algeria and Mali."

Ahman's eyebrows furrowed. "Algeria is possible because parts of the huge province of Illizi are open to off-highway traffic. One area you may check is The Tadrart Canyon, which is part of the Tassili n'Ajjer plateau. I'd stick to that area. There's a risk of over-border incursions to kidnap tourists the other ways." He finished his drink. "As for Mali, very few people travel overland great distances. There are some open areas, but anything north of Timbuktu is off-limits because of trafficking and terrorist activities."

Wil didn't like the sound of that. "Is there any other way?"

Ahman looked once more at Wil. "The area between East Algeria and Western Libya became known under Arab rule as Ifriqiya, an Arabized version of the name of the Roman province of Africa, but Libya is not a good place to go at this time. However, there were also Roman Africans living in the coastal cities of western Libya, all of Algeria, and northern Morocco. These may be good places to start."

"Let's start with Algeria since it's close."

"I'll talk to my people in the morning, and maybe we'll get started after lunch."

Chapter 17

When Wil came down to the hotel lobby, Ahman was waiting for him, and he looked excited.

He hurried over to Wil when he saw him. "Great news for you. There is a Roman city that was called Cirta in eastern Algeria. It is located in the commune of Bni Hamden in the Constantine province. The town boasts an old gate, baths, tanneries, and even a sanctuary dating back to the Fourth Century BC, along with a Christian chapel from the common era."

Wil eyed him. "Can we visit it?"

"Yes. Yes. The remnants can be explored at an authentic Roman site called *Res Eddar* or the 'Peak of the House,' which is situated in the Gorge of the Khreneg, just north of Cirta. Visitors have discovered pottery and rock inscriptions from the Roman civilization. Everything is ready to go."

Wil rubbed his chin. "How far is it?"

"Maybe a bit more than three hours."

Wil let out a breath. "I'll gather the group together."

The vehicles traveled along a road that was bumpy at times, wide open at other times, and just plain crappy much of the time; in other words, many members of the group turned a shade of green and covered their mouths with their hands.

It was past noon when they made it to the ancient site which had been called Tiddis. The vehicles stopped, and the explorers crawled out of the vehicles, and released their breakfast in the bushes. Once everyone was ready, they headed up a trail, until they stopped to marvel at the ancient structure of a gate.

"Amazing," said Delilah, who stood next to Wil with Mitch. "Did you know this was a defensive fortification during the Roman days? Its job was to protect the Cirta or the Constantine settlement. That's why it's situated on this steep hillside because of the views over the deep canyon," she said pointing.

"I'm proud of you," Wil said. "You're becoming an expert at all of this, which is important on our trips."

Mitch slapped a hand on Wil's back. "We're just glad you're with us."

Wil turned to him. "I don't get it."

"There was a lot of talk that you wouldn't be joining us, and we were both disappointed because we knew if you were with us, we'd be okay."

They turned as another group trudged up to the site and made their way through. A mother, wearing a baseball cap and jacket, and two young girls stopped in front of the gateway. One of the young girls turned to them. "Could you take a picture of us under the gate?"

Delilah took the camera and shot some photos of the three together.

"Thank you," the mother said. "I never thought I'd get to see this. It's amazing."

Mitch asked. "Yes, it is."

She sighed. "I've been researching my family's

history for the last twenty-five years. You see, I'm a descendant of the African Romans, as they were called. They existed from the Roman conquest until their language faded out after the Arab conquest of North Africa in the early Middle Ages."

Delilah inclined her head. "Are you from one of the coastal countries that they lived in, such as Tunisia, Algeria, or Morocco?"

She shook her head. "I'm from Italy. Many Roman Africans were mostly Berbers or Punics, but there were also descendants who came directly from Rome or even the diverse regions of the empire as senators. In addition, large numbers of Roman Army veterans settled in northwest Africa on farming plots promised to them for their military service."

"Is that what happened to your descendants?" Mitch asked.

"I'm not sure. My research revealed that my descendant was part of this garrison, and that's why I'm here. I can't prove it; nor can I find any information that supports that, but I decided to bring my daughters here to at least see what it could have been like for our ancestor."

Dr. Brennan hurried over to Wil. "You guys need to see this."

Wil turned to the woman and her girls. "I'm Wil Bolton. Please join us."

They joined Dr. Brennan who was with the others in the group.

Abbie was excited at what they found. "Look at this—the main buildings discovered during the excavation process. They occupied the eastern slope, and there's a door bearing ornaments that gives access to the city. We also discovered a paved road that leads to I don't know where."

The lady with them piped in. "There used to be a market here, so maybe that's where the road led to."

Abbie turned to her. "It's a possibility. And look at the upper terrace that has three open rooms, but none of them have a connection to each other. The one thing that stands out is the fact that all three are facing east."

Abbie took off and gestured for the group to follow her. Delilah grinned at the two young girls. "She's an archaeologist."

They laughed. "We understand."

Abbie pointed to the water tanks. "All of these water tanks reveal that there wasn't a constant source of water. But the inscription on the cliffs dated from the third century appears to celebrate the process of collecting water. It's safe to say that these ancient Roman ruins are one of the most remarkable findings of the region."

~

Wil heaved a breath when Holloman appeared from around the corner with two guys beside him.

"I'm glad we finally found you, Wil. You sent us to a different location."

Wil eyed him. "It seems like we meet once again."

'We do." Holloman grinned. "The three of us are going to stick around and see what happens here. You may need help finding a treasure, or once you find it, you'll need help bringing it out of its environment."

Wil sighed. "We're just fine. How about you go your own way, and we'll go ours."

Holloman shook his head. "I believe we'll stay with you. You're pretty good at finding stuff, and I wouldn't want to miss that big treasure."

Wil rolled his eyes. "We wouldn't want that now, would we? How about you and I do some searching away from the others?"

Holloman grinned. "That may be a good idea, but to be safe, I'll leave my two partners with your group in case they should find something. We could help."

They turned as Vivian brought the GPR.

"Will you look at this?" Holloman said. "We'll be able to search much better now."

Abbie gazed over at Holloman. "A GPR can locate artifacts and map features without any risk of damaging them. It's also able to detect small objects at relatively great depths. Once finished we can analyze the data."

Mitch took the controls and continued along the area around the bricks.

"Let's try over here," Wil said.

Mitch shifted directions. Vivian stood down the hill a bit studying an area of stones. "Look at this, Wil."

Wil hurried over to where Vivian was pointing. "It looks like some kind of a crack or something in the area between the stones, and it isn't in the dig area. Let's follow it."

The three followed the path and came to a rocky area along a hillside. Holloman joined them while the others went in a different direction. Wil bent down and started poking around in the brush. He jumped back at the sound as a sandpiper lunged forward.

"Get back, Wil," Vivian said.

Three sandpipers came slithering toward them ready to strike. Just like that all three disappeared into the rocks.

"What the heck was that about?" Vivian asked.

They turned to a man's voice. "Some believe they are guardians of a treasure in this area. No one has ever found out," Ahman explained.

Wil gazed at Vivian who nodded. "Are you game, Ahman, to check it out?"

He grinned. "Let's see what we can find."

"I'll follow close behind," Holloman said.

The foursome looked around for some sticks of sorts. Once found, they started poking around in the brush to make sure there weren't any more snakes. They had started walking down a hill when ten minutes later, Wil stopped.

"Is that an opening?" Vivian asked.

Wil ran his fingers through his hair. "It sure looks like it. Why wouldn't someone have seen this?"

Ahman replied, "Sandpipers. Everyone is deathly afraid of them and for good reason. One bite means almost instant death."

Wil inched toward the opening with Vivian staying close. He stopped and eyeballed her.

She grinned. "If something happens to you, I'm running the other way."

When the four reached the opening, Wil bent down to take a look. He pulled his flashlight out of his backpack and shined it around the opening. "It appears to be a cave or something along those lines. That's impossible in the desert, isn't it?"

Ahman nodded. "Not impossible. We're in a hilly area. Are you going in?"

Wil tightened his lips from the insects and cobwebs and crawled in. Ahman followed, then Vivian, and finally, Holloman. They crept for about two hundred feet when the crawlspace opened into a small room, and his flashlight shone on something bright. He pushed to his feet and held the flashlight on the sight so the others could see. It was a wide-open area that was maybe twenty by twenty five feet and rocky ground.

"What is it?" Vivian asked.

Wil grinned. "We may have found our treasure." He bent over to examine the shiny object while the other three noticed all kinds of items sprawled around the floor, specifically in one corner of the cave.

"I can't believe it," Ahman said. "Those are Roman artifacts, that's for sure."

Wil sifted through the treasure with a stick he found lying in the rocks. "Hold it, these aren't just Roman artifacts. This is a coin I've seen before — a Vandal coin from Carthage, and this looks like a small statue of an actor. Could it be Carthage also?"

"Maybe," Ahman said. "Look at the other statuette. Is that the statuette of Victoria? This is amazing, Wil."

Vivian's eyes lit up. "What's that in the corner, Wil?"

Wil shined the flashlight in the direction of her pointed finger then hurried over to examine them. One artifact was a broken Roman sword, and the other was a Roman helmet, and inside it were coins. Wil took a deep breath. "These are coins commemorating the assassination of Julius Caesar. The head shows Brutus or an ancestor, and the opposite side shows two daggers, like the ones that killed Caesar as well as the liberty cap worn by former slaves."

"Are you sure, Wil?" Vivian asked.

"I'm not positive, but it sure looks like it. Let's move these treasures out of here." Wil put the artifacts next to the wall into his backpack while Holloman and

Ahman shut the treasure box and carried it out of the cave. They had made it to the opening when the skies darkened, and the wind started to pick up. Wil turned back to the others. "A sandstorm and a huge one. We need to reach the others."

Vivian rushed past him. "I'll gather them and meet you three at that wall over there. It may provide us some cover."

"We'll need something to cover us," Ahman said.

"The tents are in the vehicles. Let's set the treasure over by the wall and gather what gear we can."

Holloman and Ahman made it to the wall and raced toward the vehicles. Wil was in the back grabbing the tents and as much water as he could, handing them to Ahman. The two hurried back to the wall where everyone had gathered, including Jessica and one of her girls.

"Isabella is still out there," Jessica said.

"Where?" Wil asked.

The worried mother pointed to another area of the wall. Wil turned to the others. "Take cover, and I'll go find her."

Jessica grabbed Wil's arm. "Please find her!"

Wil ran over to the area she'd pointed at as the winds became stronger. He had a hard time seeing where he was going but thought he heard a scream. He stopped to listen, then saw movement. Was that a person? He raced to the area and found the young girl shaking in a corner. "Isabella, we have to seek cover."

"I can't walk. Think I broke my ankle."

Wil lifted the girl up and tried to carry her back to the rest, but the wind was too strong, and the sand was too heavy for the eyes. He dropped down next to a set of bricks, dove into his pack, and pulled out some scarves. "Put this around your eyes and mouth, and whatever you do, don't pull them down."

She did as he asked. He followed suit and hunkered down into the bricks, pulling her toward him, and covered her up. "We'll have to wait it out here."

Chapter 18

Holloman stayed near the treasure to keep an eye on it. No way was Bolton going to get away with this find. His eyes landed on two men, and then met the eyes of a man he'd never seen before, and that was the last thing he saw.

Abraham gestured to Mitch. "Help me tie him up. We have to move him out of the way, or we'll never get out of here alive."

"What about the other two?" Delilah asked.

"I've tied them up also, so it will give us some time to get out of here once the storm blows over."

"How did you know?" Abbie asked.

Abraham continued tying up Holloman. "I saw them searching around and figured they were looking for Wil. I had been briefed on who Holloman was and what he looked like. When I saw him with the two guys, I slipped out of the way in order to catch them off guard. All three have been taken care of, and I also called the pilot. He's on his way as we speak and will be able to land once the storm clears."

"That means we have to head to the airstrip at the bottom of the hill," Abbie said.

"It does, but we have a head start because

everything's loaded except the treasure. I would be loading it right now, but you can't see at all out there, so we'll have to wait until the storm subsides, then we'll have to move quickly. I gave all three a knockout drug, but it'll only last for a couple of hours, and then they'll be awake, but hopefully we'll already be on our way."

Vivian smiled. "I'm glad Wil decided to bring you along."

"So am I." He smiled back at her.

~

Wil and Isabella held each other tightly as the sandstorm beat down on them. It lasted for an hour, then it was gone. Wil pulled down his mask and scanned the area to make sure everything was safe. Once he was sure, he pulled down Isabella's scarf. "We made it through."

She didn't easily let go. "Thank you, sir. I was scared to death."

"You're okay now. How bad is your foot?"

"I know for sure I broke it." "May I?" He bent down and gently felt her foot, noting that it had swollen. "We have a nurse with us who's good at what she does. She'll help you." Wil stood, lifted her up, and carried her to the others who were digging themselves out from the sandstorm.

When her mother saw them, she and her daughter raced over to her. "Isabella, are you okay?"

"Just a broken foot, I think, but I'm good. Mr. Bolton saved my life."

The mother reached up and kissed Wil on the cheek. "Thank you so much, Mr. Bolton. I'll never be able to repay you."

"She needs the nurse to set her foot. I'll set her down on this rock. Help her keep the foot elevated until I get Vivian." Wil hurried to find Vivian and check on the others. He noticed everyone was pulling the tents down. "Vivian, I need your help."

She turned to him. "There you are. Are you okay?"

"Yes, but the young girl has a broken foot."

"Let me grab my first-aid kit, and I'll check her out."

While she ran to the car to grab her kit, Wil checked on the others. They seemed to be faring well, and the treasure was still where it was supposed to be. But then where would it go in a sandstorm? He caught up with Abraham. "Don't let that treasure box out of your sight. Have Mitch help you load it into one of the vehicles, preferably the one you and I will be driving back."

Abraham looked at him. "You don't trust Ahman?"

Wil wiped his forehead. "It's not that. I'm just going to make sure it's not out of our sights. I see what you did to Holloman. What about the other two?"

"They're tied up also but not for long. The drug will wear off soon."

The two of them lifted the box and carried it to one of the vehicles, then loaded it into the back.

Wil wiped the sand out of his hair. "Once we get the young girl taken care of, we'll head back to Tunis and get this out of the country."

Abraham scanned the area and turned back to Wil. "There is an airstrip in Cirta. I called him, and the pilot should be here soon."

"Good idea." Wil hurried over to help the others. Vivian was bandaging the young girl's foot. He stood nearby and watched.

"Will she be okay?" her mother asked.

Wil listened as Vivian explained that a doctor would have to set the foot since it appeared to be a compound fracture. "I'm sorry."

Jessica took a deep breath and stared at her vehicle that was buried in sand. "How are we going to make it out of here?"

Wil said, "Where are you heading back to?"

"We're staying in Tunis. My husband is there."

"We'll take you back to Tunis and your husband."

Meanwhile the group began to dig the woman's car out of the sand and pushed it to a firm pathway.

The woman turned to Wil. "Thank you for your offer, but we can take her back to Tunis ourselves."

Vivian looked at her. "Ma'am, it would be better to get your daughter to a doctor as quickly as possible."

As if on cue, a plane flew overhead, heading toward Cirta. "There's our ride," Wil said. "Let's pack up and hit the road." He turned to Jessica. "Are you sure you don't want Isabella to join us?"

The mother sighed. "All right. Please do. She needs help soon."

Wil lifted the girl up and carried her to the vehicle containing the treasure. Once everyone was loaded, they drove toward the city airport.

They had driven ten minutes when suddenly there were several explosions that seemed to come from the ruins.

"What is going on?" Vivian asked.

"I have no idea," Wil said. "Let's move on."

They arrived at the plane, quickly loaded everything onto the plane, and were set to take off.

While they waited, Mitch said, "Do you know what's happening, Tyler? Holloman is tied up in the ruins. How did he find out we were here?"

Tyler, who had long blond hair, glasses, was piloting the aircraft. "It seems a guy in Tunis with a wife and two daughters told him about this excursion for a bunch of money."

Wil sighed. "Let's get in the air and head home."

Tyler grinned. "We're out of here, Wil."

Wil hurried back to the others and looked for Isabella who was with Vivian. "Isabella, can we talk?"

When she nodded, Vivian turned to Wil. "Do you want me to leave?"

"Nope, we're good." He turned to Isabella. "What does your father do?"

Isabella looked disgusted. "As little as possible. The only reason we came here is because a man paid our way."

"Do you remember the guy's name?"

Her eyes blinked. "Holloway or something like that."

"Do you mean Holloman? How did he know your parents?"

Isabella's eyes furrowed. "He knew that Mom was looking for her long, lost ancestors and had heard about our trip here. The man helped out."

"Do you remember anything else?"

She placed her hands on her legs. "Just that Dad told Mom she needed to find a guy named Wil Bolton and cozy up to him. And that's you."

"Thanks."

When Wil started to walk away, her voice stopped her. "My mom and sister are dead, aren't they?"

That I can't answer."

"Thank you for saving my life."

Tyler's voice came over the loudspeaker. "Wil, we have a problem."

Wil hurried to the cockpit.

Tyler pointed down at the ground. "The plane had just crossed from Algerian airspace to Libya when two fighters flew toward them aiming drones toward the plane.

"Can we shift back to Algerian airspace?"

"It may take a few minutes, and the Libyans might decide to blow us out of the air as we stand."

Wil's eyes widened. "Would they dare to do something like that?"

Tyler looked at him. "In a heartbeat, and damn what the United States thinks. What they don't realize is that this baby has a little bit more power and speed then they're used to."

"Then take us home, Tyler."

After Wil returned to his seat, the captain came over the speaker telling everyone to buckle up because the ride would get a little bumpy.

They hadn't even buckled in when the plane quickly gained speed and headed toward the Mediterranean with the Libyan fighters on its tail.

Everyone looked out their sideview windows and saw the water straight ahead of them. Just like that the plane soared to a higher altitude, and they were out over the sea heading to Europe.

Once the seatbelt went off, Wil sat down by Vivian who was still working on Isabella.

A worried Vivian asked. "What are we going to do about the young girl? She was telling me about her

grandparents in Rome."
    Wil smiled at both of them. "Get her foot fixed."

Chapter 19

Once the plane was miles away from Libya, Tyler called him and said the Libyan fighter jets had retreated. They probably returned to base once the plane they were chasing was out of their airspace.

"That was close," Abbie said, sitting down next to him.

Wil stretched out. "It was, but we're okay now. The next stop is Rome to drop off Isabella with her relatives." Abbie rubbed her temple. "I've never been to Rome. How about a day or so to check out the city?"

Wil thought about it for a moment. "I'd love to, but we have to transport this treasure back to the states. Anything can happen with Holloman around."

"You think he had something to do with the explosions?"

Wil shrugged. "It's possible."

When the plane landed in Rome later that day, Vivian, with Isabella's help, had phoned the girl's grandparents to have them meet them at the airport.

Wil joined Tyler. "Fuel up, and we'll be ready to go as soon as possible."

"Got you, Wil."

Wil returned, and he and Vivian helped Isabella

into a wheelchair, then pushed her out into the terminal to await Isabella's relatives.

Twenty minutes later, Isabella lifted her hands in the air when she saw them, then wheeled herself over to the white-haired couple. They hugged each other. Wil and Vivian followed and listened to the greetings. Wil could tell from their expressions their smiles were forced.

The man gave her a hug. "We're so happy you all made it out alive," Isabella's grandfather said.

"Are my parents and sister okay?"

They didn't answer right away, then they knelt down and held their granddaughter's hands. "We have no reason not to believe they're not okay."

As Wil settled in his window seat on the plane, Abbie joined him. "Did you get a hold of Boris?"

"I did, and I told him the approximate time we'll land. He's already throwing a big social gathering tomorrow night with press and a banquet. Boris always wants to go high class with everything."

Wil laughed. "That's Boris. I will say this excursion went much better than the last."

She laughed also. "Yeah right, we were almost shot down by a Libyan fighter plane, there were explosions, almost a whole family died, and we were hit by a blinding sandstorm."

"All in a day's work." Wil grinned.

~

The Treasure Paradise plane landed at Chicago O'Hare Airport early in the morning. They stepped off the plane into the snow with wind blasting in their face.

The weary travelers walked through the terminal and straight to two vans that were waiting for them to take them to their hotel. They climbed into the vans and arrived at the hotel an hour later.

Wil opened the door to his hotel room, and on the bed was an invitation to a social event at the Loe residence later that night. He dropped it on the bed and crashed right beside the note and was fast asleep. A couple of hours later, he woke up and called Kelsey.

An excited Kelsey answered the phone. "Are you okay? I hadn't heard from you in a while, so I thought something had happened to you, and Amanda didn't know anything either."

Wil yawned. "Sorry, still a little tired. I'm good. We just flew into Chicago a couple of hours ago, I would have called you, but I fell right to sleep."

"I'm sure you needed it. How did it go?"

"We found some Roman antiquities—a sword, a Roman helmet, plus some gold and other treasures."

"Wow, that's cool. How do you deal with everything that goes into finding a treasure?"

"I don't really think about the treasure; I'm more about the adventure. For instance, we battled through a good old sandstorm for an hour. I couldn't see a thing in front of me. And then there was a teenage girl who was lost, and we found her."

Kelsey sighed. "I'm just glad nothing happened to you."

Chapter 20

When the vans that would take them to the party showed up at the hotel, the group, obviously still suffering from jetlag, crawled in, and headed to Boris Loe's mansion. They arrived thirty minutes later. They all noticed the decorations, could smell the different food aromas, and people laughing and having a good time. Several gathered drinks.

They turned at a soft tap of the microphone. Boris Loe stepped up to the podium. "Good evening, everyone. Another wonderful artifact find, and I would like to describe what we've found. Then after that, you can view the artifacts, followed by food and drinks." He lifted up the broken sword. "This sword is a gladius, which was the primary sword used by Roman soldiers because of its short, double-edged blade for close combat. It was used from the third century BC to the third century AD, and as you can imagine, it was lethal." Murmurs arose from the crowd.

"Boris ran his fingers down the top part of the sword. "This knobbed hilt helped provide a solid grip for the Roman soldier. Stabbing was an efficient technique because stabbing wounds, especially in the abdominal area, were almost always deadly. Also, the sword was used for slashing or cutting." He held up the next item. "Here we have a galea, which was a Roman's soldier's helmet. As you can see, there is a crest holder, which is usually made of plumes or horse hair. The crests possibly were painted in yellow, purple, black, or a combination of these colors." The crowd stirred.

He glanced at the helmet and then at the other objects. "It's kind of interesting that evidence points to legionaries having their crests mounted longitudinally, while centurions had them mounted transversely." Boris reached back and pulled up a coin off the table. He smiled at everyone. "Now this is the most exciting find. It's the Ides of March coin. We not only found one but also four others, which is rare indeed. Recently, this coin sold for two million at an auction."

The hum of the crowd's response increased. Boris looked like he was salivating at the sight of the coin. "What a find! This coin was issued by Marcus Junius Brutus between 43 and 42 BC to commemorate the assassination of Julius Caesar on March 15, 44 BC. When you come up here, notice its interesting features. For instance, the front side features a heroic portrait of Brutus, the man who played a key role in the death of Caesar. The inscription casts him as a military victor." He held up the coin for all to see. "The flip side depicts two daggers which symbolize Brutus and his co-conspirator, Gaius Cassius. Also, there is a Phrygian cap, associated with freedom and traditionally worn by emancipated Roman slaves."
Boris paused. "A couple of other things. This coin commemorates one of the most crucial moments in western history and represents the overthrow of a brutal

dictatorship and the celebration of Rome's freedom from tyranny."

Wil chuckled that Boris was excited about the find.

Loe grinned. "Now that I've shared with you all this great news, I need to tell you there may be a problem. Only three known specimens of this golden coin exist worldwide, and they've been on display at the British Museum for over a decade. There is a slight possibility that these coins are a hoax. We shall soon find out."

Once the presentation was completed, many headed to the stage to view the artifacts. Security guards stood near the table.

Boris joined Wil who was standing against a wall.

Wil grinned. "Way to burst their bubble, but I'm pretty sure the coins are not original."

Boris frowned. "So am I, but still it was a great discovery. I'll know for sure in a couple of weeks. On a good note, we have two pieces of artifacts to place in the gallery, and the treasure we found is worth at least ten to twenty million. You'll receive another million dollars for your efforts."

Wil's mouth dropped. "How can you justify that much money above what you pay me?"

"It's worth it because of what you've helped find, and also the hope is it will keep you interested in what we're doing."

Wil sipped his drink. "The money doesn't interest me, but the adventure surely does. This trip wasn't too horrible. We did run into Holloman and his crew, but Abraham took care of him pronto during the sandstorm."

Boris's eyes widened. "A sandstorm?"

"Yep, it lasted an hour or so and completely covered the ruins we visited. Abraham tied the three guys up and helped with our escape in the Treasure Paradise airplane. He was a good hire. Actually, they all were good hires. They did a good job."

Boris slapped him lightly on the shoulder. "You did a good job as well."

The two looked around the room, then Boris remarked, "Treasure Paradise has turned out to be much more than I expected. I've been thinking about the next adventure which could happen over the summer."

Wil stirred his drink. "What are you thinking?"

Boris searched the room. "For sure, working with Archaeological Synopsis looking for Viking artifacts, but I'm also working on an adventure in South America along the Amazon River basin."

"Whatever happened to the hunt in South Dakota?"

Boris laughed. "Your friend is a shyster. He tried to tell me about this fossil find when I came to find out it had already happened, and he wanted my name associated with it so he could get the credit."

Wil grinned. "He's not my friend. Remember, I told you we almost ended up in a Mexican prison because of his drug dealings?"

Boris laughed. "True. Anyway, that's out. Are you on your way back to South Dakota tomorrow?"

"I am, but then I have to fly to Raton, New Mexico, for a wildlife-biologist interview."

"You're really into this, aren't you?"

"Yeah, it's what I've always wanted to do with my life."

He stared at Wil. "If you're truly interested in being a wildlife biologist, why don't you work for me?"

Wil rubbed his neck. "I didn't know you were into that."

Boris set his drink down on a tray. "I'm into a lot of things that people don't know about. I have an environmental consulting firm based out of Denver, Colorado, and Atlanta, Georgia. Both work with projects related to environmental-impact assessments, habitat restoration, and conservation planning. I need a wildlife biologist who can contribute their expertise to these initiatives. You'd be perfect."

Wil sighed. "You're involved with a lot of businesses."

"I am, but I believe in these projects. You would play a crucial role in managing a balance between human development and the natural environment that would include habitat assessment and wildlife survey, mitigation planning and regulatory compliance, species-specific surveys, and ecological impact assessment, to name a few. We're talking a $75,000 and above salary to start with, moving expenses, and of course a wonderful health plan. Think about it." He bowed his head and disappeared to another part of the room.

A voice sounded behind Wil. "You got me again. That's twice you've had the upper hand. Where did you get Abraham from?"

Wil turned to Holloman. "He was with the Army and retired a couple of years ago. Yes, he was a good hire, but then they all were. I see you made it back?"

Holloman laughed. "Yeah, Jessica who we paid to stay close to you untied us. She was a nice lady, but her husband was a dirtbag."

Wil eyed Holloman. "What about those explosions?"

Holloman grumbled. "Again, I have no idea how that happened. We were still tied up when we felt the first shaking from an explosion. No explosions went off at the ruins, so I don't know what was going on. At times while we were tailing you, it felt like we were also being followed."

Wil sipped his drink. "That tells me there's another player hunting treasure—someone who doesn't hesitate to kill."

"It sounds like it."

Wil examined Holloman. "Have you ever thought about joining our group…for real?"

Holloman laughed. "After what I've done to your team, you're asking me to join you?"

"Yeah, I understand you're doing your job, but you're good at what you do, and it would be a benefit for us, plus you'll actually make some money instead of playing second fiddle."

Holloman frowned. "You don't know Hank Lawrence. He doesn't accept failure, and I wouldn't be surprised if he had a hand in the death of that family."

"You think he'll come after you?"

He shrugged. "His wife wouldn't allow it."

Wil tilted his head. "How would you even know?".

Holloman rolled his eyes. "We've been very close over the years."

Wil grinned. "Oh, so that's why you won't join our group."

"That's one good reason, plus I do receive benefits and bonuses from Lawrence from other things that I do for him. This treasure-hunting gig isn't the only one. My guess is—after this one Lawrence will find another person, a less scrupulous one— to lead his treasure-hunting group."

Wil sighed. "Why doesn't he just let you do your job, and quit making you chase us down? Go find another treasure."

Holloman laughed. "That's how he's always done business. He waits for someone to make a mistake, then swoops in to be the hero. Lawrence will find your weakness, and he'll use it against you. Remember, Kelsey is his daughter and, despite what you believe, he still holds some influence over her."

"She and I are over. Besides she's with this Bradford guy she's known for many years."

Holloman eyed him to see if he was sincere. "Yeah, she's always liked him more than any other guy. I should qualify that—other than you."

"Don't be. It's probably for the best. I'd never fit in with her family."

Holloman laughed. "Really, no one does. I should be going. It's been wonderful talking to you. I probably won't see you at your next gig, but I'm sincere when I give you this piece of advice: The person Lawrence sends after you won't be as nice, so be careful."

Leticia Loe, Boris's wife, joined Wil and placed her arm into his. "I'm glad that your team made it back okay. It sounds like you didn't go through as much danger as the first one."

"It was much better, but then I didn't have to worry about always looking over my shoulder."

Leticia released her arm from his. "I thought I saw Holloman talking to you a few moments ago. He always comes to these events."

Wil shrugged. "Yeah, it was him. It seems like we're becoming good friends right now."

Leticia eyed Wil. "Always be alert with that guy."

"I plan on it." He changed the subject. "How do you know Vivian?"

She finished sipping her drink. "Wow, it's been a few years. Before I got married, I was sick with something they couldn't figure out, and Vivian was the nurse who took care of me before the doctor saw me. We built a friendship over the years, and she's always been part of Boris and my life. She would be a wonderful doctor, but she preferred to stay in the nurse's field. I kept pushing her to earn her medical degree and had even told her we'd pay for her education, but she still said no. Maybe you can talk her into it."

Wil grinned. "And lose her in Treasure Paradise? No way."

Leticia laughed. "I can understand that. You plan to stick with Boris on these treasure hunts?"

"Yes, but I'm also applying for a job as a wildlife biologist."

"Boris had mentioned that, and it sounds like it won't interfere with Treasure Paradise; especially if you join his group."

"He kind of offered me the job."

Leticia sighed. "Wil, Boris will do anything he can for you. He thinks a lot about you and your capabilities. I can't think of one other person he's felt that way about."

"I respect him also. Well, I should get going because I'm flying back early to Rapid City in the morning."

Chapter 21

Wil grabbed a taxi back to the hotel. He nodded at the desk clerk, then took the elevator up to the third floor and headed to his room. As he was preparing to open the door, a voice stopped him. "Mr. Bolton, can we talk?"

He turned to an older man who was shaking like a leaf. Was he drunk or did he have some kind of disease? "I don't know you."

"Of course, you don't, but I know you. Please, it's important."

Wil opened the door, and the guy followed him in. He turned to the man. "Are you okay?"

He nodded. "I'm just scared. My sister was killed by those people, and I'm afraid they're coming after me."

Wil's eyes raised. "What are you talking about?"

The guy leaned against the wall, his face pallid. Wil reached over and grabbed a cup of water, keeping the guy in his sight at all times. "Here, try this to calm down."

He took several sips of water, but it took a moment for his hands to stop shaking. "Thank you. My sister is the gal who was at the ruins with you in Algeria."

Wil's ears perked. "Explain?"

The guy took a deep breath. "I was the one who approached Xavier Holloman to talk to my sister's husband because he's been involved with some scrupulous things in the past. My reason for talking to him was to help my sister acquire some money to get away from the asshole. However, it didn't work because he ended up killing her and my niece."

Wil focused on the man. "You know that for sure?"

The man nodded. "Now he's after me."

"Is it because you knew he killed them?"

The man was sweating. "Yes, but it's more than that. The man is involved with a major international organization that also searches for artifacts. Problem is they are more lethal than even Lawrence's' group."

"You know Hank and Ben Lawrence?"

"Yes, through Holloman, who introduced me to them at a party here in Chicago. I wasn't always this whacked out, but this guy who killed my sister has me freaked out. His organization doesn't hesitate to tie up loose ends, and I'm a loose end."

"Why are you here? I can't protect you."

The guy's eyes darted around the room. "They're going to destroy Treasure Paradise and everything associated with the organization."

"This is something I'll have to deal with now. Thanks for letting me know about it."

Wil and the guy walked down to the lobby together. Once he made sure the man was in a taxi, Wil hopped in one of his own and had him drive straight to Loe's mansion. It was around eleven when Wil pounded on the door.

The butler opened it and rolled his eyes at Wil.

"Mr. Bolton, this is unusual for you to be here this late."

Wil sighed. "I know. Is Boris around?"

"The last time I saw him he was up in the gallery. I can bring you up to him."

Five minutes later when the butler announced their presence, Boris turned to Wil who stood at the door. "What brings you here late at night?"

Wil surveyed the area. "Can we talk in private?"

Boris could see apprehension on Wil's part which was unusual. "Sure, join me in the gallery conference room." Once the door was closed, Boris eyed Wil. "What is going on with you?"

He took a deep breath. "I don't know what to think about what I just heard. A guy cornered me in the hotel tonight telling me about this international group whose mission is to destroy Treasure Paradise."

Boris's eyebrows lifted. "Do you believe him?"

"He wasn't drunk, but he looked horrified, and worse off, he said this man killed his wife in Tunis."

"The same gal whom you met at the ruins in Algeria?"

Wil nodded.

Boris scratched his ear. "That's easy enough to find out if he's telling the truth. What's his name? I'll get on that first thing in the morning."

"He didn't give me his name other than he's related to Jessica."

Boris examined the gallery and then turned back to Wil. "This doesn't surprise me because of our successful finds with Treasure Paradise. Now everyone wants to get in on it, and it'll get tougher, which means I'll have to rethink how we deal with this group for everyone's safety."

"I'm heading back to the hotel and then to South Dakota in the morning. Let me know what's going on?"

"I'll do that. Are you going to be okay?"

Wil took a deep breath. "I'd rather deal with it head-on than have to worry about people doing something behind my back. That's why I'm here. I have faith that you'll do the right thing. My suggestion is to beef up the security for this team and for your business ventures. There's a mole within your ranks who is providing information to others."

"I'm beginning to wonder about that. I have a tight security system, but so do the other groups we're dealing with. I'll have to do a better job with my businesses, especially with your group of people, since you're on your own most of the time."

"I'll do what I can to make sure nothing happens to any member of the team."

Boris slapped him on the back as they walked to the door. "I have no doubt about that."

Chapter 22

Kelsey was eating lunch when she felt the cool air on her arms from the door opening. Was it Wil?

It wasn't. The man had a cold, deadly stare, and the gun he held in his right hand made him even more terrifying. "Ms. Lawrence, thank you for bringing me right to Wil Bolton's cabin. It's the only way I could get in without him figuring it out."

Kelsey did the best to remain calm because right now she was scared. "Eli Grafton, what are you doing bursting into Wil's cabin?"

"Your father sent me to take care of Wil and bring you back to the family. He misses you a lot." He pointed his gun at the security agent who came out of the bedroom. "Back off, or I will kill you. Drop your gun."

The security agent did as he said. The killer turned toward Kelsey's voice.

She had no idea why she said it. "I can always call the sheriff's department."

This made the man laugh. "You have no idea who I am, do you?"

Again, Kelsey tried to calm herself down. "I know who you are, but I am asking you to leave."

The man continued laughing. "Ma'am, I can't leave before I do what I came to do. It just wouldn't be good business."

She made a snarky remark and again she had no idea why she said it because this guy would harm her. "Then why don't you just kill yourself??"

Grafton growled. "Wil Bolton is just as important as you are, Kelsey, maybe even more important. He's the only person who can save you."

Kelsey sighed. "If you think he'll give you what you want for me, you're crazy. He could care less what happens to me."

Grafton looked at Kelsey. "Tie the security agent up, or I'll kill him."

Kelsey grabbed the tape and rope that Grafton had taken out of his backpack, tied the security guard up, and placed a piece of tape over his mouth, all the time hoping he understood she was sorry. She noticed Grafton always kept an eye on the security guard. "Now you sit down in the chair, so I can tie you up."

She did that, and Grafton tied her up. After he was finished, he stared at her. "Then why are you here, if you don't think he cares?"

Kelsey thought about her answer. "It's really none of your business and I'll tell you again, I don't know where he is."

Grafton pulled out his cell phone, turned his back on her, and called someone. After some discussion, he finally said, "Yes sir, I'll do that." He turned back to Kelsey. "Let's try this again. The security guard is of no concern to me, so either you tell me where Wil is, or your friend here won't last another minute." Grafton turned his pistol toward the security guard.

"Hold it," Kelsey said. "Let him be. He has nothing to do with any of this."

Grafton glared at her. "Are you going to tell me where Bolton is?"

Kelsey shook. "I don't know where he is."

Grafton turned and shot the security guard between the eyes. His head fell backward.

She screamed. "I told you he had nothing to do with any of this."

His cold eyes told her it wouldn't matter. "He was going to die because he had seen my face. Now where is Wil Bolton?"

"Are you looking for me? Drop the gun or I will shoot you."

The man spun around and laughed. "You can't shoot a man in cold blood."

Wil didn't take his eyes off him. "Eli Grafton, I know you've heard of the Castle Doctrine that allows a person to kill someone in order to protect their home—for instance, if there were a forceful and unlawful entry into one's home."

Grafton continued his cold stare. "Wrong. Kelsey let me into your cabin."

Wil's expression remained the same. "Any deputy who joins us will figure out that she was forced against her will, considering she's tied up in a chair. There are several other elements of the law we could talk about, but it would take way too much time, so either you drop the gun, or I will shoot you."

Grafton's guffaw left him as the bullet entered his arm and knocked him down.

Wil hurried over to him and kicked the gun away from him. "Now tell me what part you played with

Lydia Boone?"

Grafton stared up at him. "That was more than two years ago, and really, do you think I'd say anything to you about that?"

Wil focused on Grafton. "I think you would because Kelsey's father has said you're the one who orchestrated everything, just like you did to the poor guy who you dumped in Pactola Lake."

Grafton shook his head. "That was business; in fact, both were just business decisions. Kelsey knows that her father arranged the hit on both individuals. I just happened to carry them out for a ton of money."

Wil moved over toward Kelsey. "What about cattle?"

"That was quite a unique venture for your brothers. Of course, that was all about money too. You see your family and Kelsey's family are making tons of money, while you struggle here in this cabin."

Wil sighed. "You're telling me Kelsey knew you were coming to kill me today?"

Grafton rolled his eyes. "Of course not. I came for both of you. She would have lived if you had joined Kelsey's father's treasure-hunting group. If not, I had orders to kill both of you."

Wil continued. "Again, her father ordered a hit on his own daughter?"

Grafton frowned. "Of course, he did. Who do you think I work for? However, there is one person above Hank Lawrence that you'll never figure out because even I don't know about him."

Wil sat down on a chair. "Why would you tell me any of this stuff? Do you have an exit strategy considering I have you under the gun, as you say?"

Grafton laughed. "Of course, I do. Hank Lawrence never leaves any stone unturned. I don't see any law-enforcement officials here, and the reason for that is because he has them under his thumb, or in this case, in his pocket."

"So, I should just let you get up and walk away?" Wil cocked his head to the side.

"It would probably do you good, but the problem is I'd have to come back and do it again."

Wil stared at him for a long moment. "Eli Grafton, you're not going anywhere but to the Lawrence County Jail and then to prison for murder and attempted murder, along with several other felonies that the district attorney will deem necessary."

Grafton's laugh waned as the sheriff and district attorney came out of the other bedroom. Grafton's eyes widened. "Hold it, you can't do this."

Wil eyed him. "Sheriff, explain to him that no one forced him to talk."

Sheriff Kanter nodded. "That's kind of what I heard. Of course, Mr. Grafton, you can have Hank Lawrence's attorneys try to make bond, but he could be too busy trying to keep himself out of jail."

The district attorney added, "Besides, we have a witness who saw you shoot the security guard in cold blood. I'll push for the death penalty, which will hold up because the guy's tied up."

The door opened, and the deputy stood just outside. "Take him away, deputy," the sheriff said.

~

Wil turned to Kelsey and untied her ropes. Her eyes were frightened. Once she was free, she jumped into his arms. "I knew you would come for me. I'm so sorry the security guard died because of me."

"He didn't die because of you, Kelsey. Like the district attorney said, Grafton is a vicious killer, and neither one of you would have survived. His orders were to kill you."

After everyone left, Kelsey sat outside on the porch bench. Wil brought out a blanket and sat next to her. "It is cold tonight," Wil said.

Kelsey wiped tears off her face and peered up at Wil. "I've caused so many problems for you, but you're still there for me. Why?"

"You keep me on my toes."

She laughed. "How did the sheriff and you get in the house without me knowing it?"

He took a deep breath. "Remember, we put in that back door after this situation with the brothers?"

"Right. I was so scared I couldn't think straight."

Wil stood up. "Let's get something to eat."

She grimaced. "How could you be hungry after what just happened?"

He winked at her. "I hoped he'd hurry up and confess to what he had done because my stomach was growling. Let's go to Rapid City."

The two headed there, then Wil pulled into a mall parking lot and parked next to a steakhouse. "I hope this is okay. I've had a craving for a nice steak for a while," Wil said.

"This is wonderful," Kelsey said. "I'm fine with a steak."

The two sat down and placed their order, then Kelsey gazed at Wil. "A question for you — are you CIA or something like that?"

Wil laughed. "Far from it. When I was in high

school, I joined both the archery club and the gun club, and that's where I learned how to become proficient with a bow and arrow and a gun. I was never in the military or worked for the CIA or FBI, or anything of that magnitude."

"Bows and arrows? Now I feel really safe." She sipped her water.

"I also joined the scouting programs where I learned how to live in the outdoors, which was where I decided I wanted to be a wildlife biologist. At Frostburg State, I took a lot of biology and science courses that I loved, although I didn't like them in high school. Go figure."

She leaned forward. "I didn't like science in high school either. That's why I chose fashion instead."

"Well, I probably would have liked it if I'd studied more. My family life wasn't the greatest. Tessa and I had always been very close, but Del and Cole have never liked me and vice-versa. My parents were hard to explain. They always wanted more money, and they were fortunate enough to inherit a few millions after Mom's parents died. Many believe my father found a way to screw the other siblings out of their share, but it could never be proven."

She took a nibble of the salad the waiter had brought as Wil was talking. "So, you're as genetically challenged as I am."

He sighed. "You'd be right. I was twelve when Tessa had Maddie, and I remember holding her when she first came out. Cliff hadn't made it to the hospital yet. The little thing kicked and giggled at me, and we've been close ever since. When Maddie was five, Tessa and Cliff moved to Seattle because she earned a wonderful job in the banking industry, and that's where she met Brandon. The two spent more time together than they should have, partly because Cliff wasn't the same guy she'd married, and she was lonely."

"Why did she move to South Dakota?" Kelsey asked.

"Maddie missed me and wanted to be close to me, and Tessa was trying to pull her life together knowing her marriage to Cliff was nearly over. I don't know what happened to her and Brandon, other than he moved to Chicago."

Wil stopped when they delivered their steaks. As they were eating, he continued. "I did have a few girlfriends in high school, college, and then Lydia, when I first moved to South Dakota. The reason I moved to South Dakota was to work in my chosen field, but that didn't pan out. Hampton had hired me to be a wildlife biologist, but the government cut some funds, and one of those positions was the wildlife-biologist position. He did hire me to chase down wildlife tracks and rescue goofballs who veered off the designated paths and got lost in the Black Hills."

Kelsey put down her fork and leaned her chin on her fist. "Wow, you've had an interesting life."

Wil grabbed his drink. "One time I guided a group of scientists into the northern hills searching for some kind of dinosaur fossil, and that's when I first became interested in searching for artifacts."

"How did you and Lydia connect?"

"She worked at a casino in Deadwood as a bartender. One night at least three guys hit on her and asked her out for dates. Lydia brought me a beer and said, 'I'm so sick and tired of being hit on by drunk men.' She started to walk away but turned toward me and asked, 'why haven't you hit on me?' I didn't have an answer for her. A couple weeks later, I was back in the same bar, and the same guys hit on her. She told them, 'I don't think my boyfriend would appreciate your continuous hitting on me.'

"They asked, 'Who's your boyfriend?' She pointed to me, and that's how it started."

The two were quiet as they finished their dinner. As they waited for the waiter to bring the check, Kelsey asked, "I dated boys here and there, and then when I was twenty-one, I met your brother, Cole, and we hit it off. We dated for a year, and for the first time, I felt like things were different for me. I was wrong."

"Drugs?" Wil said.

She nodded. "I didn't know it until it was too late. He was distributing drugs out of Chicago during that time, and he was rich. I met him at one of those ritzy social banquets that we're always attending. We danced together and then started dating. Then I found out my father used him to distribute drugs and diamonds through my clothing shipments. I figured it out from what you told me."

Wil grinned. "You decided to listen to me for once?"

She smiled. "Yeah, I did and I'm glad."

"How did that happen?"

"A friend of mine overheard them talking and said something to me about it. It pissed me off, so I decided to dig deeper. You know, I wonder if Cole was the one who had those guys attack me?"

Wil covered her hand with his. "Anything's possible with my brother."

After he paid the bill, they headed out to the vehicle. Wil opened the door for her. "Feel like taking in a movie with me?"

Kelsey yawned. "I'd rather go back to the cabin."

They made it back to the cabin after ten-thirty. Kelsey stood and peered at Wil. "I enjoyed myself tonight. Thank you."

Wil smiled. "Me too. Oh, I forgot to tell you. My sister is marrying the deputy sheriff in Arizona this weekend, and I plan on heading out there. Would you like to join me?"

Kelsey eyed him. "I'd love to if it's not an inconvenience."

She could see Wil's blue eyes glowing. "No, it's not. I'd love to spend nights under the stars with you."

Chapter 23

The next morning Wil and Kelsey packed the truck for their trip to the south.

Kelsey finished sipping on her coffee. "My boss was really nice about allowing me to take the week off, especially after I told him I was traveling with you," Kelsey said. "This will be a unique trip."

"It's awfully hot down there during the summer months, but in January it'll be much cooler. At night it gets cold, so we'll have to snuggle in."

Kelsey grinned. "I plan on it."

The two drove down Nemo Road and onto Highway 385 to Deadwood, then to Lead where Wil connected with Highway 85 and headed south toward Denver, but first they continued climbing into the Black Hills.

Kelsey stared out the window at the snow-covered hills. "This is beautiful."

"We're at O'Neil Pass, elevation of more than sixty-seven-hundred feet and the highest paved road in South Dakota."

"I can feel it," Kelsey said.

Wil glanced at her. "Are you okay?"

She was a little red. "Yeah, I'll be okay once I

catch my breath."

The snow started coming down gently at first, but then picked up as they climbed higher. Wil watched flakes hit the car. "It seems like every time I go through here, it's snowing."

"Maybe you should try the summer months?" Kelsey grinned.

Wil smiled. "You could be right. This is the quickest route. It's the road we take to go to a professional sports game. Like tonight, we should make it in time to watch the Nuggets play."

Kelsey nodded. "How long is this pass we're on?"

Wil's eyebrows furrowed. "About twenty-five miles. It starts at Cheyenne Crossing and ends in Four Corners, Wyoming. There is a lot of wildlife in this area, and during the winter it can be very dangerous. In fact, this road is considered the most dangerous road in South Dakota."

She cut a sideways glance at him. "I've often said there'll never be a dull moment with you."

They continued the climb and then passed Trailshead Lodge, then headed down to Wyoming. They'd traveled for another twenty minutes when Wil pointed to a group of buildings to his left. Kelsey looked at what he was pointing at. "It looks like a resort of some kind."

Wil nodded. "The story is that it's a resort where members of the mob go for relaxation in the Black Hills."

"Are you serious?" Kelsey asked.

Wil shrugged. "I don't know if it's true, but I've heard several people talk about it. Who knows?"

Kelsey shivered. "I don't think I want to stay

there."

Wil laughed. "I promise we won't."

It was close to eleven when Wil and Kelsey arrived in Lusk, Wyoming, which was a halfway stop for travelers over O'Neil Pass on their way to Cheyenne, Wyoming, and Denver, Colorado. Will pulled into a gas station and started pumping gas.

Kelsey stepped out and stretched. "I'll grab us food and drinks."

They continued down the road and arrived in Denver around three and pulled into the downtown Hyatt Regency near the Pepsi Center. The two checked in and caught an elevator to the third floor. Kelsey pointed at the room number on their door.

"What is it with room 333?"

Wil shrugged. "It's brought me good luck."

She inserted the key card and opened the door. "Aw, our very own hot tub. You sure know how to travel in style."

It was close to six when the two headed toward the Pepsi Center to watch the Nuggets play the Detroit Pistons. Wil had purchased seats on the court.

After the two sat down, Kelsey surveyed the arena. "This is a perfect view of the game and, wow, are those guys tall!" she said as the players came out to warm up.

One of the basketballs rolled toward her. She picked it up and threw it to one of the Nugget players.

He smiled at her. "Nice-l-ooking gal."

She peered over at Wil and lifted her hands. "I get that all the time."

They both laughed. The game started and basically ended before the first quarter ended as Denver rolled to a 110-57 win.

After the game, they walked back to the hotel. Kelsey yawned. "That wasn't much of a game. Detroit didn't have a chance after the first quarter."

"Denver won the NBA title last year, and it looks like they may do well again this year."

Snow started falling as they neared the hotel. "This is so beautiful," Kelsey said, watching it snow. "I never really took time to enjoy snow, but for some reason when I'm with you, I've changed a lot of my perspectives on stuff."

Once in the room, Wil climbed into the hot tub, and Kelsey sat on her bed reading a magazine. "Listen to this, Wil. There are more than 56,000 recorded prehistoric sites in Colorado. That's amazing."

Wil pushed some suds away from him. "You're starting to get more involved with archaeology, aren't you?"

"Well, you're involved with it, and I want to learn as much as I can with you."

The next morning the trek continued to Utah where they had planned to spend the night in Zion National Park near St. George, Utah. They drove through the Rocky Mountains on Interstate 70 and arrived in Utah after lunch.

Kelsey pointed at a sign for Arches National Park. "Could we drive through there?"

"Sounds good." Wil turned south on Highway 191 and within the next hour arrived at the national park. As they drove, she googled the park's backcountry for hiking. "Listen to this, Wil, the backcountry consists of mostly rough terrain, inaccessible by established trails with very limited water sources." She turned to him. "Do you think we should just take the driving tour?"

Wil moved over to allow a car to pass. "We can do that."

Kelsey continued reading. "The Windows section seems to be the place to be, according to Google. It is the 'beating heart' of the park. The area offers scenic locations like North Window, Turret Arch, and Double Arch. Did you know that the arches were caused by the cutting action of wind-blown sand?"

Wil peered over at her. "I read that somewhere." Wil drove the eighteen-mile trek, and they came to Delicate Arch. They stepped out and hiked toward the arch. They both stared at the view. "They say that this arch is number one on must-see lists in this area of Utah."

Wil and Kelsey stopped, and he pointed toward the light opening beneath Delicate Arch. "That is approximately forty-six feet high, and the entire rock span is around sixty feet tall."

Wil backed up to get a better look. "Wow, look at its unique shape. That must be the reason it's strong and stable, unlike other arches that are prone to collapse."

Kelsey looked up at the top of the arches. "What is that?" she asked, pointing.

Wil covered his eyes and looked up to where she was pointing. "It looks like a nest of sorts."

Kelsey quickly googled wildlife in the arches. "It sounds like it's a white-throated swift, which is a black and white bird known for its fast and agile flight. It prefers open areas near cliffs or other structures where it can roost and nest."

"That's probably what it is. Good ole google."

The two climbed back in the truck and continued their tour.

She giggled. "I'm surprised that this old pickup of yours has made it this far."

Wil rolled his eyes. "If it doesn't, we walk."

It was towards dinnertime when they reached Zion National Park. Wil found Watchman Campground, and they pulled into the site. They climbed out of the truck and searched the area. "Fewer large trees mean less shade," Kelsey said. "But it does allow for better views of the mountain."

Wil opened the back of the pickup. "Let's get the tent set up, and then we'll go for a hike before we grill some food."

The two had the tent set up in about fifteen minutes. Wil grabbed some water and bugspray. They began the trail that headed toward Watchman Mountain.

Kelsey studied the vegetation as they walked. "Is that some type of cactus?"

Wil stopped and studied it. "Yes, it's a prickly pear cactus which grows in a hot desert environment."

They continued up to the mountain and found a rock to sit on to view the area. "Look at that view of the whole area of the park," Kelsey said.

Wil got his bearings straight. "That's the south side of the park, and there is a visitor center down below. Should we go down?"

"Please, so we can grab souvenirs."

Wil and Kelsey arrived at the visitor center thirty minutes later and did some browsing through the gift shop. He purchased a couple of books on the national park, while Kelsey bought a puzzle of the park's most famous landmarks as well as a blanket.

She wrapped it around her when they returned to

camp. "I plan on staying warm tonight."

After they finished their meal, the two sat in front of the bonfire wrapped in Kelsey's new blanket and staring at the mountain view over them. She was content. "This is so peaceful and so gorgeous. Why do you enjoy being outdoors?"

Wil thought about it. "Probably the peacefulness and the freedom to be alone. Like I said last night, my home life wasn't the greatest, and I found ways to get away from it all. This was one way to do that. I also did a lot of hiking around the Annapolis area. At times I walked around the water district just to watch the boats and wonder what it would be like to own one."

The two watched as the fire finally went out. Wil stirred the embers to make sure they were out, and the two climbed into their tent. Kelsey used the blanket to cover both of them up. She looked into his eyes. "Thanks for another wonderful day."

The next morning the two drove toward the Grand Canyon and arrived around lunchtime. Kelsey jumped out of the pickup even before it stopped. "Let's take the helicopter tour."

"Slow down."

She giggled. "I'm sorry it's just that it is so cool to see the Grand Canyon."

They climbed into the chopper and settled in for the forty-five minute flight as it lifted up into the air toward the Grand Canyon. Two other tourists were with Kelsey and Wil. Kelsey grabbed Wil's arms. She felt like a schoolgirl seeing the Grand Canyon for the first time with her first love.

The two listened as the pilot provided background about the Grand Canyon that included lying in the

Colorado Plateau of northwestern Arizona, was one mile deep and eighteen miles across at its widest point.

"We're flying over the South Rim, which is open year-round, and is the most accessible side of the Grand Canyon featuring Mather Point, Hopi Point, and Mohave Point."

The pilot explained they were flying over Mather Point, which he offered an iconic view of the Grand Canyon. "It's the one you see in nearly every photo. It's also the most crowded due to its ease of access."

As they circled the area, Kelsey asked him a question. "What is it composed of?"

"It's made of Kaibab limestone and is mostly buff or tan, white. The rock at the point is distinctive with its limestone erosion holes and is broken into large blocks. The point is more than seven thousand feet high."

As the chopper continued its flight over the Grand Canyon, the pilot talked into his mike. "Down below is Grand Canyon Village, and we will be flying over Hopi Point in a few moments. Hopi Point is another famous spot for sunset and sunrise viewing."

Everyone looked at the sight as the pilot described what they were seeing. "Hopi Point extends farther into the canyon than any other point on the South Rim. As you can see, it provides different panoramic views of the Colorado River and the canyon."

He circled closer. "See the various rock formations rising from the canyon floor? They include Shiva, Isis, and Zoroaster temples."

They ascended again and moved to a new area. "Finally," the pilot said. "This is Mohave Point which also offers views of the river and canyon's beautiful sunsets. What's cool in the morning is the way the sun lights up the river in the late morning creating a 'magical ribbon' on the canyon floor."

Several minutes later the chopper landed back where it started, and the group climbed off. As they returned to the pickup, Kelsey grabbed Wil's arm. "That was so cool."

Chapter 24

The next morning, Wil and Kelsey drove toward Mesa, Arizona. It would take about six hours of driving, but they planned on stopping at different sites along the route. As Kelsey quickly fell asleep with her head on Wil's shoulder, he continued down the road thinking about all that had happened during the past couple of days.

It was after two when they arrived in Mesa. Kelsey had slept most of the way and woke up when Wil stopped at a red light. He looked at her. "Good afternoon, sleepyhead."

She wiped the hair out of her eyes and smiled at him. "It felt good to sleep. You could have woken me up, and I would have driven."

"No, we're good. You looked so peaceful, and I didn't want to wake you. We should be at my sister's house soon."

As they pulled into a large driveway, they both marveled at the large adobe house spread out across the acreage.

"It's a fairly large and a nice-looking house," Wil said.

"It surely is. The houses are nice down here."

Wil frowned. "My old pickup truck sure doesn't fit in with all of this."

"Don't worry. Let's enjoy our time with your family."

The front door opened, and Maddie and Jonathan came running out. "Uncle Wil, Aunt Kelsey, you made it. We're so excited to see you," Maddie said, hugging Wil and then Kelsey.

Wil reached down and picked Jonathan up. "How have you been?"

"Wonderful. Wait until you see Jerald's parents. They're nice like you."

"That's good to hear."

The four walked into the house to see Tessa, Jerald, and his parents sitting on the couch. Tessa hurried over to Wil and hugged him, then she did the same to Kelsey. "I'm so glad you're here with Wil. He's missed you." She turned to an older couple. "These are Jerald's parents. Bill and Evelyn Ankler."

"Nice to meet you," Wil said.

Bill Ankler stood up and shook Wil's hand. "Your niece and nephew have been telling all about your escapades. Did you know that there is plenty of treasure right here in Arizona that hasn't been found?"

The comment intrigued Wil. "I can imagine."

"Have you heard of the Apache Tears?"

"I haven't."

Bill crossed his arms and explained. "It's basically made of volcanic glass that forms when lava cools rapidly, and it's named after the Apache tribe because they believed these stones were tears shed by their ancestors who fought to protect their land. Their unique appearance and the connection to Apache history makes them popular among rock collectors."

"Are they valuable?" Wil asked.

"They don't have significant monetary value, but they are valuable to collectors because of their cultural and historical significance."

Bill sipped on his iced tea, then offered them seats as Evelyn left the room. "There are at least four locations where it's possible to find these valuable items — Globe, Superior, Peridot Mesa, and San Carlos Lake. The last two are located on the San Carlos Apache Reservation."

"Have you found any?" Kelsey asked.

"Nope, but I do know a couple who have looked for them and have been successful."

They turned as Evelyn walked in. "Enough of your tall tales, Bill. It's time to eat."

"You know they're not tall tales, Evelyn," he said.

That night after dinner, the group sat out back at the pool. Maddie and Jonathan spent time swimming while the adults sat on lounge chairs talking.

"In two days, you'll be marrying our son," Bill said, looking at Tessa.

She nodded while she sipped her lemonade. "I'm happy about all of it. Jerald is a wonderful guy and reminds me a lot of my little brother, Wil, who is also kind and considerate." She winked at Wil.

Bill broke in. "I've heard what happened in Yosemite and Papua New Guinea, also. What's your knack for getting out of tough situations?"

Wil sighed. "I really can't explain it other than it's just something that I sense is going to happen, and I'm always thinking ahead."

Tessa interrupted. "Wil's been like that since he was a little boy. No one in the family could understand it either. He's nothing like any other member of the Bolton family."

Kelsey asked a question. "What got you into law enforcement, Jerald?"

Jerald took a deep breath. "I lost a good friend in high school who was killed by a drug sale gone wrong, and I vowed I would do anything I could to clean up drugs. As you can imagine, it's a never-ending battle, and the guess is drugs and the people who profit from them will never be eradicated, but I'll keep trying."

"That is true," Evelyn said, waving her fan to keep cool.

The group spent another hour chatting before they called it quits and headed to their respective rooms.

Two days later, Tessa and Jerald were married in a ceremony in the Ankler's backyard-pool area. Wil and Kelsey were standing to the side watching the first dance. After it was finished, Wil peered at Kelsey. "Would you like to dance?"

"I hoped you would ask me." He wrapped his arms around her and pulled her close.

"I've really missed this," Kelsey said. "Are we okay?" she said, peering up into his eyes.

"We're okay. I'm through worrying about the things you and I've done in the past. I want to start a new life, and I want to do it with you, possibly in Idaho."

"Do you think you'll get the job?"

Wil sighed. "I don't know, but I sure hope so because I want to get as far away from everything as possible."

She reached up and kissed him on the cheek. "Just as long as it's not away from me."

Chapter 25

The two arrived back at Nemo three nights later. They both were tired, dropped their bags on the couch, and headed directly to their bedrooms.

The next morning Wil was up, made some coffee, and sat outside on the porch watching the snow come down lightly. His phone vibrated, and he answered it.

"Wil, good to hear you're up this early."

Wil laughed. "Boris, it is past eight here in South Dakota."

"Just thought I'd tease you a bit. I have some information for you and Kelsey; actually, it has to do with Kelsey. Is she there?"

"No, she's actually sleeping right now, but I can wake her up."

"No, don't do that. I'll talk to her later. I am flying to Atlanta tomorrow and wondered if you could join me to talk about the job there with the environmental consulting agency; that is, if you're still interested."

Wil stretched. "Sure. Do you want me to fly directly to Atlanta?"

"Yes, I'll have a ticket available for you at the Rapid City airport. The flight leaves at nine in the morning."

"I'll see you in Atlanta tomorrow afternoon. Don't be surprised if it's raining, but at least it's not snow."

Kelsey touched Wil. "Who were you talking to?"

Wil peered up at Kelsey who was holding a cup of coffee in both hands standing in one of Wil's long t-shirts. "Aren't you cold?"

Kelsey tasted her coffee. "Nope, I'm starting to get used to all of this cold weather. I got used to it in Chicago after a while, but now I'm adapting to the South Dakota weather."

He sipped his coffee. "To answer your question, that was Boris Loe. He wanted to talk to you about something, but I told him you were sleeping. He wants me to fly to Atlanta tomorrow to meet with him about the wildlife biologist job at his environmental consulting firm."

She leaned against the door. "Are you going?"

"Yeah, and I was wondering if you wanted to join me."

Kelsey shook her head. "I can't. I have to work several days this week, and I can't continue to take days off, especially since I just started working there."

~

Kelsey decided to walk to work before he flew out. Wil had offered to drive her, but she wanted to walk. The weather was chilly but doable, and she needed time to think about her and Wil. Things were truly looking up, and they would have a future together.

It was close to eleven when she walked into the Brandin' Iron. "Good morning, Nils," she said.

He finished placing napkins on a table. "Good morning to you also. How was the walk this morning?"

"It's a little chilly, but I do enjoy the walk back and

forth to work."

Nils grinned. "Wil should get his butt out of bed and drive you here."

Kelsey laughed. "He offered me a ride before his flight to Atlanta, but I wanted to walk to think about things."

"I'm sure Wil is on your mind."

She eyed him. "Why would you think that?"

"I've known him for almost three years, and you are the only one I've ever seen him with." He continued cleaning glasses. "Your family has come to Nemo."

Her mouth widened. "They've been here."

She could tell Nils was thinking from his wrinkles on his face. "Yeah, for the past five years, I believe it's been. They meet with other bigwigs from South Dakota and the surrounding states. Strange, since this is a quiet town that not many people know about."

She frowned. "Have they been here recently?"

Nils put his glasses on. "The last time they were here was maybe a month or so ago talking to a guy I've only seen once before. It may be a coincidence, but the guy was here in the bar, and right after that, Wil's brother's friend was found floating in Pactola Lake."

Her eyes widened. "You know Wil's brothers?"

"Oh yeah, they stopped by many times. The word is they're big into the drug sales in this region, and this is one of the places they make their deals."

Kelsey stared at Nils. "Why would you let them do that in this place?"

He shrugged. "The one time I gave them a warning, they were out of here pronto. In fact, I called the sheriff's department, but they arrived too late, and Wil's brothers haven't been back since. I try to run a respectable place, but there are a lot of things that happen out here that people aren't aware of."

"I understand that. What do you need me to do?"

He shrugged. "What can any of us do?"

Later when she returned from work, Kelsey opened the cabin door and noticed how quiet it was. The house was more than empty when he wasn't here. She slipped into Wil's t-shirt, crawled into the other bed, and was out like a light.

Chapter 26

As Wil sat onboard the plane waiting to fly to Chicago, he thought about Kelsey and wished she would have come with him but understood about just starting her new job. The jet taxied, then took off, and he was fast asleep before it even got into the air.

When he landed in Atlanta, he caught a taxi and went directly to Boris Loe's residence. He knocked on the door and a tall man stood in front of him.

"Wil Bolton."

The man at the door looked over the list. "Welcome. The bar is to the right and a buffet is further down. Please enjoy yourself."

Wil walked toward the bar. He surveyed the crowded room and noticed several people he had seen before and many he'd never seen in his life. "What would you like?" the bartender asked.

He thought about it. "Rum and coke tonight." Once he had his drink, he mingled with others.

"Wil, we're glad you could make it."

He turned to the voice. There stood Harrison Bradford with Crystal, Kelsey's sister. "Nice to see you, Harrison. Crystal, how have you been?"

Crystal grinned. "Good. How about you?"

Wil took a deep breath. "Kind of tired but doing okay. What brings you two here?"

Harrison tasted his drink. "Boris and I have been working on a project together, and, well, Crystal and I have been pretty much together for the better part of a month or so."

Wil tipped his glass toward her. "I'm happy for her."

"Thanks Wil," Crystal said.

The three chatted for a bit, then Crystal eyed Wil. "Dance with me?"

Harrison jumped in, "Go ahead, Bolton, I'll dance with her for the next one."

Crystal took his hand and led him onto the dance floor. She pressed her hands against his chest.

He frowned. "What is going on here?"

She looked up at his face. "Simple, you're going to tell Kelsey to back off."

He pushed away. "I have no idea what you're talking about."

She frowned. "Don't be a liar. You know you've broken her heart the way you've treated her, and she'll probably never get over it."

Wil would never say anything about Kelsey to her family. "I'm sure she's accepted that we're not together and has moved on with her life. For sure, I thought she'd be with Harrison, but she was right in stating that you seem to take the guys that she likes."

Crystal grinned. "That's what I do. You're very good at keeping your composure, but you don't have a clue about Kelsey."

"Like I tell everyone who asks me about Kelsey, that's not a subject I discuss, so if you want to talk about anything else, go ahead—maybe the fact that your father is running scared, knowing that he's so close to spending time behind bars. I remember telling him to do the right thing for his daughter, but he must not have gotten the message."

Crystal glared at him. "He got the message, and I'm sure what he'll tell you is your time is almost up."

"That's exactly what Eli Grafton said when the sheriff took him off to a South Dakota jail for murder."

Once the song was over, Wil couldn't get away from her fast enough.

When they returned to the table, Harrison smiled. "Did you enjoy yourself, Crystal?"

Wil smiled. "I did, but now it's your turn if you feel up to it."

He stood. "I'd love to."

Once they were gone, Wil slipped out of the house, grabbed a taxi, and made it back to his hotel. He paid the taxi driver, caught the elevator, and went to his room. After sliding his key into the door, he walked in and dropped onto his bed. Of all the luck—to run into Kelsey's sister who was looking for Kelsey. He grabbed his cell phone and dialed Kelsey. "Wil, is everything okay?" she asked, after the third ring.

"I'm fine. I was calling to see how you were doing?"

"That is sweet of you. It has been a busy day, and Nils is showing me how to make some new drinks. I never knew the guy was that talented when it comes to drinks. In fact, he's thinking about making me a partner."

Wil could sense her excitement. "Wow, good for you."

There was silence on the other end. "Wil, he wants me to attend a wine conference with him in Colorado next weekend. Are you okay with that?"

"What do you think about it?"

"I'm not sure. There's a part of me that thinks it'll be good, but another part that says stay near you. Are you okay?"

"It's been a long day. Do you what you think is right, Kelsey."

"You're not okay, are you Wil?"

Wil thought about what he wanted to say to her. "I ran into your sister and they're looking for you, but I lied and told them I had no idea where you were. When it comes to you, no one will know what's happening in your life; at least not from me."

"I feel the same way about you."

Chapter 27

"Welcome back, Mr. Bolton," a lady said when Wil walked into the environmental consulting company headquarters the next morning. She had long red hair placed in a ribbon, with glasses, and a butterfly tattoo on her left wrist. She smiled. "You don't remember me from last night, but I was there helping with the social."

"Oh, sorry."

She led Wil to a conference room where Boris and others stood chatting.

Boris smiled when he saw him. "Wil, come on in and let me introduce you to a few of the people here in the Atlanta branch of the environmental consulting company."

Harrison Bradford was also there and came over to shake his hand. "Wil," he said. "Good to see you again."

"Same to you."

Boris had went to the front of the room. "Everyone, take a seat, and we'll talk a little bit about what's the next course of action." Once they were seated, he started. "First of all, let me introduce Wil Bolton, who leads my Treasure Paradise group looking for artifacts.

He has a degree in environmental science and is thinking about joining this firm." He turned to Wil. "Quickly, let me tell you a bit about what we're doing here. To make it simple, our job is to offer guidance and solutions for businesses that want to operate in an environmentally responsible and sustainable way."

Over the next hour, they discussed upcoming projects east of the Mississippi River. After the meeting was over, Boris and Wil chatted about what they'd talked about.

"Do you have any questions?" Boris asked.

Wil rested his hand on his chin. "Not necessarily questions but just some thoughts. You sure do have a lot of projects that you work on in the eastern United States."

Boris shuffled his notes. "That's true. When we first started, there were maybe one or two companies that did business with us. Now the number's grown to several dozen on each side of the Mississippi. There are a lot of companies that want to be more environmentally friendly with the land. As a result, we need to hire a number of employees."

Wil placed his hands on the table. "It's interesting and it's something I'll have to consider, but right now I'm just not sure."

Boris leaned back in his chair. "I can understand you need time. When do you plan on flying back to South Dakota?"

"Tomorrow."

"Good, why don't you join a group of us at a social gathering with some potential clients, and you'll see how everything works. It's pretty informal tonight, so don't worry about a suit and tie."

~

Kelsey stood behind the bar cleaning glasses as she waited for more customers to come in. It had started to snow, so she wasn't sure if there would be a lot of customers tonight, but then again, she had seen them pile in when the snow was a foot deep.

Nils walked in and how quiet the place was. "This would be a first where no one showed up for a drink, but then it's only seven. Have you decided about the trip next weekend to Colorado?"

Kelsey lifted her head. "Yeah, I'll probably not go. I can stay here and run the bar if you wish."

He frowned at first, then he shrugged. "That will work. I'm sorry that you don't want to see how wine is made and taste other types of wines, but I understand."

They both turned as the door opened, and a cold wind blew through. Three men hurried in and shut the door. "Wow, I believe we're going to have a blizzard as cold as it is and the wind that's blowing," one of the men said.

Another hurried to the counter. "How about something to warm up the insides?"

Kelsey smiled. "Three hot buttered rums coming right up."

"With barbecue chips," another said.

Over the next hour, the bar started to fill up. Almost everyone was talking about a major winter storm coming in.

"They're talking about at least fifteen inches of snow," one guy said.

A gal added, "The winds could be as strong as forty miles per hour. I'm staying close to home for the next couple of days. Nils usually closes this place during the major blizzards, anyway."

Nils peered up from where he was checking supplies. "The bar will still be open this weekend even though I'll be out of town. Kelsey will handle everything."

One of the guys grinned. "That's good news for all of us."

"Why's that?" Nils asked.

"She's a helluva lot prettier than you are, and what's more, she makes one wonderful hot buttered rum. In fact, I'll take another one."

Many others joined in. It was ten-thirty when Kelsey returned to the cabin. She had walked in, made herself some hot chocolate, and sat down on the couch when her cell phone rang.

"Wil, what's up?"

"A group of us are heading to California to see Laney and Bailey. Do you want to join us?"

Kelsey stretched out on the couch. "No thanks, I have to work, and it gives me more time to think about where I'm going in my life."

"I can understand. Are you okay?"

Kelsey wrapped two hands around her hot chocolate. "I am getting better, much better. Enjoy yourself, and I'll see you when you get back."

Chapter 28

Kelsey opened the Brandin' Iron at eleven the next day. Nils had left her a note that provided her with a couple of items that he had forgotten to mention, including more liquor coming in to fill up the stock.

The first customers came in at noon and ordered the special—a grilled cheese and tomato soup. Kelsey handled the bartending and serving while a young gal named Ophelia handled the cooking chores.

Kelsey knew Ophelia was only eighteen, but she did a good job of handling the food. She had a son who was a year old and had brought him to work with her many times, which Nils didn't mind. The more she knew about Nils, the more she liked him. He was only thirty, handsome, and had always been nice to her and everyone who came through the bar. It surprised Kelsey that so many people frequented the bar, since Nemo was such a small town. Nils had told her that the Brandin' Iron was a hidden gem in the Black Hills, and there were several of those hidden gems in the town that few people knew about.

Today was April first—April Fool's Day around the country. Kelsey had to laugh at some of the stupid things her siblings used to pull on their parents, but that part of her life was over.

The bar was busy throughout the lunch hour and only slowed down after two. Samuel, the liquor guy, showed up with several cases for Nils. Kelsey showed him where to unload them. She grabbed him a coffee, and they chatted for a bit.

"So, you deliver liquor as well? I thought you were a construction guy," she asked.

He tasted his coffee. "I live in Rapid City but distribute to different lounges, bars, and casinos in the northwest, along with my construction work."

Kelsey leaned on the bar. "Wide circuit."

"That's true. There's a lot of travel, but I enjoy seeing the different places. The bars are so different it's unbelievable. Most show the flavor of their community, which is cool. Like the Brandin' Iron displays photos of the views of the area. Anyone who comes in here can feel what it's like to live in this area."

"You must love traveling."

He nodded. "True. I wouldn't trade it for the world. Wil Bolton is another guy just like that."

"He is, that's for sure."

"We've talked many times about what it means to live in the Black Hills, and we both agree it's so peaceful, there is so much beauty around, and we both enjoy living life—not just putting in time for a paycheck. I'm sure there are other places like the Black Hills, but this is my home and the home of many others like me." He tasted his coffee. "That guy is a true adventurer, which is evident by his treasure-hunting. He revels in stuff like that, and he's fearless when it comes to anything remotely dangerous. I don't understand it at all. How do you know him?"

Kelsey rolled her eyes. "You're so full of it. I was there when you came over to do some work on the cabin."

He laughed. "You're right, but I never tell a lie, at least one that anybody knows about, but in this case it's the truth. Anyway, I should get going before the snowstorm strands me here in Nemo."

"Aren't there plenty of bars in Rapid City?"

Samuel grinned. "Yep, but none as cozy and quiet as this one and a few other places around the Black Hills. With you behind the bar, it makes it that much more exciting to come by."

Kelsey smiled. "Don't let Nils hear you say that."

Samuel laughed. "He's a very good boss, because he protects his employees and doesn't take any crap from us. You have a wonderful night."

Kelsey laughed as she took his glass and placed it in the dishwasher, which she usually had to run several times each night because of all the beer people drank. She had suggested Nils just buy bottles of beer, but he said that cost too much.

It was about eleven when she finished cleaning the bar, then she started the truck and made her way back to the cabin. She was already missing Wil, and he had been gone only a couple of days. Kelsey had no clue how she'd handled it when he was gone on his treasure hunting trips.

After Kelsey pulled into the driveway, she locked the truck up and walked into the cabin. She grabbed herself some hot chocolate and sat down on the couch. Just then a figure walked out of the bedroom.

"Wil, what are you doing here? You scared me to

death. You're supposed to be in California."

He sat down next to her. "I couldn't do it because I wanted to spend time with you." He lay down, resting his head on her lap.

She set her hot chocolate down and stroked his hair. "I'm so glad you're here because I entered this empty house and already started to miss you."

Wil peered up at her. "Are you feeling better?"

"Yes. I enjoy working at the bar and could do it for a long time depending on what you do." She bent over and kissed him. "I want to be with you. Hope you feel the same way."

The next day at work, Kelsey spun around when the door to the Brandin' Iron opened and the wind blew through. Everyone else in the bar looked up as well when Wil hurried in and headed toward Kelsey. "Is everything okay?"

His eyes were wide. "The blizzard is socking the southern hills down near Hot Springs; they're trying to get everyone out of certain areas and into Hot Springs for safety. A couple of families are stuck in areas that they can't get to, so they've asked us to try to get them out."

Kelsey touched his hand. "Please be careful."

He peered into her eyes. "I'll be back. Here are the keys to the truck, so you can get home safely. The blizzard will be here soon."

She watched as Wil hurried out the front door. A few moments later she heard the swish of the helicopter blades and hurried over to see it lower in an open area away from the Brandin' Iron. She watched as Wil climbed into the chopper, and it lifted off.

A hand touched her shoulder. "Wil will be just fine

because he's in his element."

She turned to face Samuel and smiled. "That he is."

165

Chapter 29

"What do we have?" Wil asked Caleb.

Caleb turned back to him. "At least three couples are still stranded in cabins. Three summer cabins where the owners came back earlier than normal. In two of the cabins are older people, and in the third cabin is a young mother and her two children. She's involved in a messy divorce."

Wil reviewed the map in front of him. "It looks like there is only one place we can land the chopper to reach two of the cabins. The third area where the woman and her two children are going to be a bit more difficult. We'll have to lower me down in a rope."

Caleb frowned. "Last time we did that you had to run from a fire. There has to be another way."

Wil continued studying the map. "There is an open area maybe a mile, mile and a half away, which we could travel inland to reach them."

"That's what we'll do," the pilot, Reese Winters, said. "We'll grab the two families, and I'll bring them back to Hot Springs while you two grab the gal and her kids."

Caleb turned back at Wil. "Are you okay with

that?"

"Let's do it."

An hour later they had reached the two couples, who now sat in the helicopter, and Reese landed the chopper in an area where Wil and Caleb could jump down and head into the hills. "I'll be back as soon as I can, and I'll be waiting right here," Reese said.

Wil and Caleb hurried in the direction of the cabin, which was just over a mile away from the landing area. The snow and wind were strong, but the trees helped block some of the wind, but the snow was still deep in certain areas of the hills.

Caleb turned to Wil. "What was this gal thinking about coming here with two kids?" Caleb asked.

He shrugged. "Maybe she was doing what she could to get away from a crappy situation."

The two continued on. Wil stopped and peeked toward the north at a faint outline of a house. "There's the cabin. It doesn't look like there is anyone there at all."

"That can't be, at least according to what we've been told. Let's check it out."

Wil stopped. "Isn't that Bailey Blue's old cabin?"

Caleb looked up. "It sure is."

The two arrived at the front door, and Wil knocked on it. "We're here to help you. Is there anyone there?"

No sounds. Wil tried to open the door, but it was locked. He kicked the door open, and the two hurried in. There was no heat in the cabin. He headed to the back bedroom, and lying in the bed was a woman and two young children. The three had wrapped themselves in blankets the best they could to stay warm.

"Are they still alive?" Caleb asked.

Wil touched her to see if she had a pulse. "Barely." He did the same to the children. The youngest girl, who may be about one, smiled at him. "This one seems to be just fine. The other one is okay also."

Caleb radioed what was happening, and Amanda answered, "They have a doctor ready at the Hot Springs clinic, and Reese is heading to the rendezvous area as we speak. You have to hurry because the blizzard is picking up and is spreading across the entire Black Hills. Things are shutting down everywhere."

"Copy that," Caleb said.

He hurried over to Wil. "You heard all of that?"

Wil nodded. "I've bundled them the best I can, but for sure the lady will have to be carried out of here. We'll have to switch off, and I'll carry the young lady if you grab the kids."

"We just have to move."

Wil wrapped the lady up in a blanket and slipped her over his shoulder while Caleb grabbed the two children, one under each arm. They hurried out of the cabin and toward the open area where the chopper would hopefully be waiting.

They stopped a couple of times to switch, and then they heard the blades of the chopper. They came out of the forest just as the chopper started to set down.

"Wow, look at that wind!" Caleb said. "Reese is having a hard time keeping it upright."

When he finally set the chopper down, Wil and Caleb loaded the gal and the two kids.

Once they were on, Reese struggled to lift the chopper up and had trouble keeping it in the air. "This wind is stronger than any I've ever encountered."

Caleb was back working on the lady. Wil was in

the seat next to Reese. "Is there anything I can do to help?"

Reese grinned. "Pray." He kept the chopper in the air and headed toward Hot Springs. They landed at the Fall River Health Services twenty minutes later. Two nurses were waiting there for the crew, and Will and Caleb helped the nurses with the gal and her kids.

"Do you know who they are or anything about them?" one nurse asked.

"No ma'am," Wil said. "We do know they were in Bailey Blue's old cabin, but we're not sure what significance that may have."

"We'll take over from here."

Wil and Caleb sat out in the waiting room until Reese hurried in. "Anything?"

"Not yet," Caleb said. He turned to Wil. "It's strange that she would be at that cabin. Did you know that Bailey sold it?"

"No clue," Wil said. "But we can find out." He stepped out and called Laney.

She answered after a couple of rings. "Is that really you, Wil?"

He took a deep breath. "We rescued a lady and two kids from Bailey's old cabin here tonight during a blizzard. Do you know if he sold the cabin?"

"He sold the cabin to his twin brother not too long ago. Why?"

Wil found a place to sit. "We just rescued a gal and two kids, and the kids look exactly like Bailey."

"That would make sense because Brody and Bailey are identical twins. I've met his wife and the two kids, but never her husband."

Wil closed the phone down. Caleb looked at him.

"Well?"

"Bailey has an identical twin."

Chapter 30

Kelsey stood behind the bar watching the group of people who were sitting at the tables. The blizzard had stopped, but roads were still closed, but it didn't stop the hearty group of South Dakotans who needed their drinks. Most came by snowmobiles.

"I'll take another one of those hot buttered rums," one guy said to her.

She had served plenty of drinks during the afternoon. The customers were also talking about the blizzard and the rescues that had occurred during the last day.

Samuel sat at the bar and ordered a beer. "Kelsey, how are you doing today?"

"I'm doing well, and yourself?"

He tasted his beer. "Good. I think I've helped at least half a dozen people dig themselves out of snowbanks that they would have never been in if they had just stayed home."

"What makes people think like that?" Kelsey asked.

He shrugged. "There are so many people who want to see what's happening during blizzards that they don't think about their own safety. I hear the chopper group made some heroic rescues."

Kelsey's eyes widened. "Chopper group?"

Samuel laughed. "Yeah, Wil, Caleb Streeter, and Reese Winters are three guys who do the craziest damn things to save people. They landed in an open area, and two of them traveled more than a mile to rescue a mother and her two little girls. No idea what happened to the mother and girls, but the guys are just fine. I thought you would have heard about that."

"Not a thing," Kelsey said, cleaning out some glasses.

"Now you have, and you can pass it on to others who ask about it."

Kelsey laughed. "I've found out that bars are the best place for a gossip session."

He swilled his drink. "Right, it's the best place to find out who's with who. Everyone's asking who you're with because they don't know."

She frowned. "It's really none of their business who I'm with."

Samuel swallowed his throat. "That's true. Whoever the guy may be is very fortunate because you are a nice-looking gal."

She grinned. "Thanks, but again, don't let Nils hear you say that."

"Say what?" Nils said, coming over.

Kelsey grinned. "Samuel enjoys the beer that you import from other countries."

"That's good to hear."

After Nils left, Samuel frowned. "I can never learn to close my mouth. Sorry."

~

Wil remained in the waiting room in Hill City. He

felt good about Kelsey, and he decided he should just move forward with her.

"Wil, you're still here?" The doctor headed toward him.

Wil stood up. "Is she okay?"

"They're all going to be okay. The problem is I have no idea who her family is because she won't talk about it. Would you know about her?"

"I don't know anything."

"We did find out her name is Courtney Willis, if that's her correct name, so at least we have something to start with."

Wil stood up. "Can I talk to her?"

The doctor nodded. "Sure, I don't see why not since you saved her life. Perhaps she'll be happy to talk to you."

Wil walked back to the room she was in.

The young gal stopped sipping her juice and turned to Wil when he walked in. "Are you the guy who saved me and my children?"

"One of them."

She sighed. "I should say thank you, but I wished you wouldn't have."

Wil's eyes widened. "Why would you think something like that?"

When the gal clammed up, Wil sat down in a chair next to her. "You have two adorable children."

She smiled at that. "Thank you. It's too bad their father is such a jerk."

Wil sighed. "I don't expect you to respond to this, but they look just like a friend of ours, Bailey Blue, who now lives in California."

She hesitated for a moment. "No, his twin brother,

Brody, is the jerk I was talking about. We were married three years ago, and then I found out he was married to another gal, which isn't valid anyway because we never were divorced. What an asshole!"

"I don't know what to say about that, but it's important that you tell the nurse about him so they can figure this thing out."

"Believe me, I plan on it."

Chapter 31

"Hey Wil, Amanda, we're having a potluck this weekend and we want you to join us at the house."

"Sure, what do you want me to bring?"

Amanda thought about it. "Whatever you want, but basically yourself. We'll have a big crew here. Also, the sheriff wants you to stop by his office. He has some news for you."

"I'm on my way."

Wil pulled into the sheriff's parking lot in Deadwood and strolled into the reception area.

The receptionist peered up. "Hi Wil, I'll get the sheriff."

"Thanks."

Sheriff Kanter walked out a few moments later. "Come on back. Will you grab us two coffees?" he asked his office administrator.

While the two were chatting, she showed up with the coffee and closed the door behind her as she left.

The sheriff grabbed his coffee. "I received a call the other day from a Mr. Kelley from Salmon, Idaho, who is checking into your background."

Wil nodded. "Yeah, I applied for a job as a fish-and-wildlife biologist up there."

Sheriff Kanter leaned back in his seat. "I knew that was your field of study. We sure will miss you when you leave."

Wil shrugged. "I haven't got the job yet."

"From our conversation it sounds like you're their top choice."

"We'll see."

Wil had stepped out of the sheriff's office when his cell phone rang.

"Good morning, this is Mr. Kelley. Is this a good time to talk?"

Wil sat on a bench outside the office. "Sure, we're good."

"Great. We're into the second round of interviews, and you've made the cut. This weekend we're bringing all the finalists in to meet and greet with the public, employees of the forest service, and the board members. It's a weekend affair, and we hope you can make it with your significant other."

After he left the office, Wil called Kelsey who was working at the bar. She answered after the second ring.

"Is everything okay?"

"Yeah, it's fine. I received a call back from Mr. Kelley in Idaho, and he wants both of us to join him this weekend. Are you up to it?"

"I wouldn't miss it. I'll ask for time off.

~

Later that afternoon, Wil and Kelsey drove toward the Streeters' house. The sky was overcast and there was a chance they may receive some type of moisture anytime.

She slid over next to him and took his hand. "I've missed you, but then I always miss you. What about

Treasure Paradise and Idaho?"

"I've had time to think about that also, and I have a feeling I'll be just fine. It'll take some work on our ends, but we can do it."

She looked at the dessert sitting next to her. "You actually made this chocolate cake?"

"Yeah, it's actually for Reese because he loves chocolate cake, but the others will dive in if they have a chance."

Kelsey laughed. "Are you saying Reese may eat it all?"

"That's what I'm saying."

They arrived at the Streeters' house, the curb crowded with cars and trucks. Kelsey turned to Wil. "I remember how busy this place gets."

Wil let out a breath. "Yeah, anytime there's a party, people get excited."

When they entered the house, the first people they saw were Caleb and Reese. The living room was smaller than many but it fit the Streeters.

"You two made it," Caleb said, shaking his hand and hugging Kelsey. Reese did the same thing.

"Is that a chocolate cake?" Reese asked.

Wil grinned. "It is. Or at least it's my attempt at making a chocolate cake."

"My favorite," he said, taking the cake away and hurrying to the kitchen.

Wil and Caleb laughed.

"What was that all about?" Kelsey asked.

Caleb grinned. "The guy is a little different, but he's a helluva pilot."

"That he is. There sure are a lot of people here," Wil said.

Caleb smiled. "And a special guest showed up specifically for you."

Wil's eyes widened. "What are you talking about?"

Caleb stepped back and pointed. Wil glanced over at Laney who was talking to Amanda and another gal. "What's she doing here? Where's Bailey?"

"I'll let her tell you about it. This may be quite awkward for you."

Kelsey touched Wil's arm. "Don't worry about me. I'll be okay."

They turned as Amanda and another gal hurried over to them.

"Wil, it's good to see you," Amanda said, hugging him. She turned to Kelsey and did the same thing. "Come join us with the ladies. We have more important things to talk about."

She laughed, and the two gals dragged Kelsey with them.

~

Wil joined Caleb in the kitchen. They had to laugh when they saw Reese was there with chocolate cake all over his face.

Reese laughed. "Wil, this is the best chocolate cake I've ever had. Try some."

"Is there any left?" Caleb asked, laughing.

Reese looked around. "Sure, there is, but there may not be for long if you don't hurry."

Caleb frowned. "We haven't eaten lunch yet."

Caleb turned to Wil. "That's your responsibility to cook the brats, dogs, and hamburgers."

"Lead me to the grill."

Caleb and Wil stepped out back to the patio, "I'll bring out the food to grill," Caleb said.

Wil started the grill and stared at the backyard as he waited for the food. He turned to see Laney heading toward him with a platter of raw meat.

"I'm the designated food-bringer," she grinned.

Wil took them from her and set them down on the table, then he pulled her near him and hugged her tightly. The two had been friends ever since Wil had arrived in South Dakota. "It's so good to see you," Wil said. "Where's Bailey?"

She returned the hug just as tightly. "What are you doing back here?"

"Long story, and I'll tell you about it later. Right now, I'm here to help you grill some burgers, brats, and hot dogs."

After they were done grilling, they brought the food into the house. Wil headed into the living room.

Kelsey grabbed plates for the two of them and brought them to Wil. She frowned. "Is everything okay?"

"I need to get away for a moment." Without waiting for her reaction, he headed to the front door.

"Where are you going?"

Wil stared at Laney. "I need to go for a walk."

"I'll join you."

Before Wil could say anything, she linked her arms with his. The two walked along the bridge over the creek and stopped at a bench that Caleb and Amanda had set up to look over the creek. They both cleared off the snow and sat down.

"It looks like the ice is starting to melt," Laney said.

"It is."

Laney took Wil's hands. "I know you want to

know what's going on."

Wil rolled his eyes. "It came to mind."

She took a deep breath. "I wanted to talk to you in person about my feelings toward you. I was going to tell you when you were in California, but you didn't show up. I did care immensely about you before, but once I hooked up with Bailey things changed. I love him, and we are having a child together, so I hope you're okay."

Wil watched a bird fly away. "I'm fine, Laney. Kelsey is a wonderful gal, and with her I can start my life over, which I need to do."

Laney squeezed his arm. "What does that mean?"

"Just what I said. For so long my life has been about the past, but I've never looked to the future. I hunt for treasure, and now I have a chance for a new job in Idaho with a gal who is happy just being with me. You were the only other one who ever made me feel like that, and I'm so happy for you. I wish you the best in your life."

"Now I feel much better because we've talked it over."

Wil grinned. "I really hate drama."

Laney laughed. "How about we join the others before Caleb and Amanda think we did something we shouldn't be doing."

Chapter 32

"You know we could have flown to Salmon," Kelsey said.

Wil eyed her as he drove down the road. "But you wouldn't have experienced the scenic drive through Wyoming, Montana, and Idaho, and of course the snow."

"How can I forget the snow? But you're wrong because it's June and most of the snow is gone by now." Kelsey grinned.

Wil put on his blinker to pass a car. "It's a ten-hour drive from Rapid City to Salmon, Idaho, but I wanted to stop at the Little Bighorn, a grizzly bear compound in Montana, and maybe a couple of other places."

Kelsey giggled. "Oh, did you expect us to go around searching for treasures on this trip?"

Wil sighed. "Not really. That part of my life is over. I had dreamed about searching for treasures after finding the coins. And it was an adventure. I don't know if I'll continue it though."

Kelsey's eyes widened. "Why?"

"I want to concentrate on just being a fish and wildlife biologist and not worry about the other stuff. It's time to start a new life. Are you ready for lunch?"

"I could eat something, but this land is so wide open, and I haven't seen a town or even a ranch for several miles."

Wil had noticed that also. "They are few and far between. We should be coming up to Ashland in the next ten minutes, and we can find a restaurant there. After lunch, we should be at the Little Bighorn within the next hour."

Kelsey googled Ashland, Montana. "Population of less than five-hundred people and is east of the Northern Cheyenne Indian Reservation and is also located along the Tongue River."

"Any restaurants?"

Kelsey checked her cell phone. "Maggie's Cafe pops up. It looks like a nice little place. One review says, 'not fancy, but fine for a traveler's breakfast.'"

Wil grinned. "It sounds like our kind of place."

The two pulled onto Ashland's Main Street and found the cafe. Wil parked the truck, and the two walked into the restaurant. It wasn't that crowded, but he could tell they were strangers because of the stares they were receiving.

A young Native American girl joined them and handed them a menu. Wil looked up at her. "What's the special today?"

She smiled. "Grilled bison loin with caramelized strawberries."

"I'll take that with water," Wil said.

Kelsey stared at her menu. "I'll have the cedar-planked salmon," Kelsey said. "Also, with water."

The server took the menus. "I'll be back in a few minutes with your meal."

After the server brought them their drinks, Kelsey

sipped her water. "Tell me more about your thoughts about Treasure Paradise and now this wildlife-and-fish biologist job? You can't do both."

He took a deep breath. "I enjoy the treasure-hunting bit, but I want to get completely away from all the politics involved with it. We go places and Hank Lawrence has his men following us, and there is a second wildcard that nobody can figure out at this point. It's much simpler to work in my profession, something I've always wanted to do."

She took his hands. "I can understand that, but please realize who you are. You are the adventurous soul that loves to explore, hunt for things that educated people want, and see different places around the world. There aren't many people wired like you are."

Wil studied a bison photo on the wall. "Look at where it's got me? Gals who don't want anything to do with me, people who are either shooting or burying me alive, and family members who can't leave me alone."

Kelsey studied the room, then turned to face Wil. "Just know that I'll support whatever decision you make. Right now, I want to enjoy my meal."

The two finished eating and drove toward the Little Bighorn Battlefield, arriving at the cemetery plot an hour later. They climbed out of the pickup, Kelsey grabbed pamphlets at the trading post, then they walked up the paved sidewalk to the gravesites.

She linked her arm into his as they stood at the top looking over the graves.

"It's kind of eerie the way the wind is blowing, and yet it's so quiet up here," Wil said. "The battlefield has become a place of reflection and serves as a memorial to those who fought in the battle."

Kelsey read the brochure. "More than a thousand Native Americans and members of the 7th Cavalry died at the site on June 25 and 26, 1876." She shielded her eyes to look around the area. "With all the rolling hills, I can see how the cavalry was surprised by the Lakota, Cheyenne, and Arapaho warriors. It was a tragedy."

They both stood quietly just watching the scene for another thirty minutes. Kelsey started shivering, and Wil pulled her close to him. "Are you ready to go?"

"I did catch a chill, but I'll stand here with you until you're ready to go."

Wil squeezed Kelsey. "I'm just thinking about what the soldiers felt like when they came out of those draws and saw a slew of Native Americans waiting for them." Wil pointed to the area. "Coming over any of those hills had to be a freaky situation, and although many were slaughtered, the calvary showed a lot of bravery. I couldn't have done it."

She peered up into his eyes. "I disagree. You'd be right there with them, but the difference is you'd find a way to survive because for some reason you have that survival instinct most people don't have."

They stood there another twenty minutes before Wil finally took Kelsey's hand, and the two walked down the hill toward the pickup. It was past one when they left the Little Bighorn Battlefield.

"Where to next?" Kelsey asked.

"We can stay in Bozeman and visit the Montana Grizzly Encounter where we'll see bears in a safe environment."

Kelsey smiled. "I can deal with that."

They arrived at the Montana Grizzly Encounter at four and found out it closed an hour later. "We made it just in time," Kelsey said.

They stood with a group of people listening to the guide who talked about the grizzly-bear rescue and education sanctuary founded in 2004. The guide said, "Not only does it provide a spacious and natural home for rescued grizzlies, but it also offers a place for the public to learn about their way of life."

Kelsey took pictures of the grizzlies and asked another couple to take photos of her and Wil together with a grizzly bear in the background. They were fortunate as the bear lifted onto its back two legs, and the shot showed him hovering over them, but from twenty or thirty yards back. She showed Wil the picture. "That is so cool. We can show everyone that we survived a grizzly-bear attack."

Wil rolled his eyes. "Yeah, right."

Kelsey giggled. "Let's grab some souvenirs."

Kelsey purchased a sixteen-ounce ceramic mug with a classic outdoorsman look for each of them, a couple of children's books about bears, and two Montana Grizzly Encounter hoodies.

They found a hotel in Bozeman, grabbed dinner, and then drove to the Museum of the Rockies. They walked into the museum, and Kelsey picked up a brochure. "This museum supposedly houses the largest collection of dinosaur remains and the largest Tyrannosaurus Rex skull ever found," Kelsey said. "Wow, it is huge."

A guide responded to her comment. "Ma'am, the museum is renowned for its extensive collection of dinosaur fossils. If you come this way, I can show you fully reconstructed skeletons and bones and egg nests."

Wil and Kelsey followed the guide to several spots.

"This is amazing," Wil said. "Look at how cool they are."

The guide continued on. "A walk through the history of the universe in this planetarium shows the history of the earth and the life that emerged from the Mesozoic Era through lifestyles of the Natives and European settlers until after World War II."

Wil and Kelsey spent another couple of hours touring the facility before driving to the Bozeman Hot Springs to soak their worn-out bodies.

Kelsey tested the water in several of the different pools until she found the one she liked and lowered into it. "Over here Wil, this pool has the perfect temperature."

Wil joined her and both leaned against a side rail. "This is perfect."

Kelsey pointed above. "I love the lighting, and the fact we can move to pools with different temperatures until we find the right one." She looked around. "And maybe it's just tonight, but it doesn't seem too crowded."

Wil put his arm around Kelsey, and she held his hand. She peered into his eyes. "This was a wonderful day, but I am getting tired, and tomorrow we have another four-hour drive."

"I'm with you."

Chapter 33

Friday morning, Wil drove onto Interstate 90 and headed toward Salmon. They made several stops along the way for the picturesque views of the Rocky Mountains. Wil pulled into Salmon after one o'clock. After they pulled into the Stagecoach Inn where all the activities were being held, they climbed out of the truck and stretched their legs and arms.

They noticed the river several hundred feet away. "Look at the Salmon River and Bitterroot Mountains," Kelsey said. "It's so beautiful."

Wil reached into the back and grabbed the baggage. Kelsey returned to help and took one of the suitcases. They entered the inn, and the gal at the front desk greeted them with a smile.

"We're here for the weekend activities with the national forest service," Wil said.

"Very good," the gal said. "Here are your room keys, as well as complimentary tickets for one drink tonight and tomorrow night. There is a free breakfast buffet tomorrow morning, which is something specifically for this weekend."

"Thank you, ma'am," Kelsey said.

After they checked into their room, Wil and Kelsey

joined a group of others sitting in the back at tables where people could sit and enjoy the view of the Salmon River and the Bitterroot Mountains.

Wil and Kelsey leaned against a brick wall that surrounded the property looking at the somewhat frozen river. They turned to a voice.

"Wil, you made it?" Mr. Kelley, who was the manager of the fish-and-wildlife service, stood just a bit shorter than Kelsey's five-nine height.

"Yes, we did. Mr. Kelley, this is Kelsey Lawrence."

He stuck out his hand. "Nice to meet you, ma'am. We're happy that you could join us for this social gathering this weekend. This is something new we're trying with all five finalist candidates and their families. As you can see, some of the finalists have children, and others brought their parents with them. It should be a wonderful weekend."

"Thank you, Mr. Kelley," Kelsey said. "We look forward to it."

A lady with graying hair and walked with a limp joined them. "This is my wife, Barbara. We've been married for thirty-seven years now."

She smiled. "Thirty-seven wonderful years, I might add. Nice to meet you two."

"You too," Wil said. "Ma'am, what is your part in all of this?"

"Wow, no one has ever asked me that question. Most talk to my husband about such things, but since you asked me, I'll tell you it is important for the staff, the board, and community members to get a chance to meet the people who will be part of this community. The Frank Church-River of No Return Wilderness is such a unique area and needs people who will do their best to help preserve it."

Wil grinned. "Very eloquently spoken. You must have heard your husband say those words many times."

They all laughed, and his wife nodded. "You would be right, Mr. Bolton."

"Please call me Wil."

"And you can call me Barbara. I would like to stay and speak with you more, young man, but we have others to visit. Can't let anyone think we play favorites." She winked at him.

Once they left, Kelsey linked arms with Wil. "She's a nice lady, and he seems to be a nice man."

An hour or so after mingling with the other families, Mr. Kelley invited the group into the hotel for a buffet meal. Wil and Kelsey followed an older couple through the buffet line.

The guy, with red hair and freckles, proffered his hand. "I'm a member of the board and you are?"

"Wil Bolton, and this is Kelsey Lawrence."

"Right, you're a candidate for the fish and wildlife biologist position."

"Yes, sir."

The guy spread his arms out. "What do you think of all of this?"

"The view or the event?" Wil asked.

"A little bit of both."

"First, it's a great idea to have something like this where everyone can get to know the community and people associated with the area, but of course, that's something Mr. Kelley had mentioned during the interview process and tonight. Personally, it gives me a chance to find out what's expected of me by talking to board members and especially the community members." He grabbed a plate and handed one to Kelsey, then continued. "We both realize that this area is all about the ecosystem, so we need to make sure we preserve the integrity of the area. More importantly, we need to work with all entities involved, so they'll buy into whatever plan is made to preserve the area."

"Nicely said," the man's wife said.

As they continued through the buffet line, Kelsey peered up at Wil. "You made an ally right here."

Wil sighed. "How come politics is involved in everything we do?"

There was a laugh from behind them. Another guy had stepped into line. "I'm sorry, I shouldn't have been listening, but I'm with you, sir, there is always too much politics in government affairs. How would you deal with that if you were with the forest service?"

"Wow, putting me on the spot in a buffet line. That's tough."

The man laughed once more. "Yeah, it is."

Wil thought for a moment. "There is no way around the political process, but my goal would be to make sure that all the staff members and their ideas are treated fairly. For example, if there is a change in policy, everyone would have an opportunity to participate and would understand what the policy means if it is changed. By the same token, if there aren't regulations, the wilderness area and the community would suffer because everything would be so discombobulated that no one would know what's what." Wil grabbed a dessert. "I hope that answers your question."

The man grinned. "It does. Enjoy your meal."

"I wonder who he was?" Kelsey asked, as they searched for a table.

"I don't know, but all these questions are interesting."

She kissed his cheek. "You're doing a good job."

He blushed. "Thanks. I'm glad you're here."

After dinner, many people went back to their rooms, but Wil and Kelsey decided to take a walk down to a path around the river. As they started their walk, they noticed Mr. and Mrs. Kelley standing against the wall looking at the mountains.

"This is so beautiful," Mrs. Kelley said, when the two walked over to them. "I stand outside our house almost every night and just stare at the mountains. It's so calming."

"I want to show you something," Mr. Kelley said.

The four walked a bit down the path and stopped at an area where they could clearly see the water. Mr. Kelley pointed below. "The Salmon River is considered sacred ground and a rich source of food for the indigenous people of the area. Salmon are also vital for the coastal community economy and also plays a critical role in ecosystem health, and that includes more than 130 animal species like the orca whale and grizzly bear." He turned to Wil and Kelsey. "This job isn't just a job; it's saving a way of life those from Idaho to the Pacific Coast. Remember that, Wil, when you start working here. Good night, you two, and we'll see you tomorrow."

~

"I've missed that so much," Kelsey said, rolling over and lying on Wil's chest. "But then I've missed a lot of things with you." She traced her index finger around his heart. "Are we okay? I mean truly okay?"

He grabbed her other hand. "We've been through a lot in ten months, more than most people go through in their entire lifetime. I enjoy everything, even the fiery attitude you have sometimes."

She stopped with her finger. "I'm trying so hard to move away from the things I've done in the past, especially the things I know that concern you, in particular, honesty and marriage infidelity. I've never thought about another guy since I've been with you."

"Even Harrison Bradford?"

Kelsey frowned. "Even Harrison Bradford. I was infatuated with him when we were younger, but no one can hold a candle to you. All I want is to spend the night talking to you, making love with you, and doing it over and over."

He laughed. "You've got it all figured out."

"Yeah, I hope so. I've missed you so much, and it hurt so badly that you and I had thought about never being together again. I must have cried for several days after that night on the pier when you said it was over. Please don't ever hurt my heart like that again."

He kissed her gently. "I don't plan on it. What made you decide to go to Sheriff Kanter and tell him the story?"

She returned the kiss. "I had told you I would do it and then didn't, so I felt if I couldn't show you that I'm sincere in turning my life around, I couldn't blame you for not wanting me in it. Is the only reason you and I are in this bed tonight because I did that?"

His eyes widened. "Not even close."

"Then what was it that changed your mind?"

Wil let out a breath. "I told Carly Sanders the only

reason you were even with me was because you wanted something from me, and this is what she said, 'yeah, your love.' Then she told me another time, 'you are making a big mistake not having her in your life. Right now, you're hurting, but if you don't marry the gal, you'll regret it someday.'" He kissed Kelsey on the lips again. "The fact that I'll regret not marrying you someday has resonated since she said it. I don't ever want to feel that."

She popped up. "Are you asking me to marry you?"

"Someday I will."

"And when that day comes, I'll say yes." She lay down on his chest. "What are you going to do about these jobs?"

"It's a wait-and-see mode right now, but I believe I have a great chance for the one in Salmon."

"Would you really accept it? And if you did, what about Treasure Paradise?"

Wil stared at the ceiling. "I'm really excited about the job in Salmon, and if they offered it to me, I'd take it. I'll miss the cabin and everything associated with the Black Hills, but we'll be able to start a new life in a new place, and that's important."

She kissed him on the forehead. "I'm with you about starting a new life elsewhere."

"How are you handling not working in clothing and design?"

"I'm ecstatic that I have the time to do things on my own. But more importantly, I want to raise our children with you, and I can't wait for that to happen."

Chapter 34

The next day, two buses took the candidates through the protected Frank Church-River of No Return Wilderness in Valley, Lemhi, and Custer counties.

The guide explained, "The wilderness protects several mountain ranges, extensive wildlife, and a popular whitewater rafting river." She sipped her coffee. "It is known as the 'River of No Return' for its swift current and large rapids, which makes upstream travel difficult. A trivia fact for you. If you've seen or heard of the *River of No Return* with Robert Mitchum and Marilyn Monroe, part of the movie was shot on the Salmon River."

The buses spent most of the day touring the area and then returned to the hotel for a dinner banquet. Wil was getting dressed in their hotel room when Kelsey walked out of the bathroom.

His mouth dropped. She modeled the dress. "What do you think?"

"Wow, you're gorgeous. What did you do to your hair?"

She lifted her hair up. "It's called a golden beige blonde. I've stayed true to my brown roots but made it sparkle with golden highlights. It's the first time I've ever done anything like this. And it's the first time I've worn this dress with knee-high boots. I wanted to be stylish."

"You are."

Kelsey grinned. "You can close your mouth now, Wil." She looked up as Wil tried to knot his tie. "Here let me take care of that." She finished it and then looked at him. "Looking pretty sharp."

"And you look gorgeous."

She blushed. "This is an important night to you, so I want to look my best."

He took her into his arms. "You realize no matter what you wear, you're always beautiful."

"You've said that before and I thank you for it. Let's go enjoy ourselves."

The two went down to the banquet. Several gathered around Wil and Kelsey to ask them questions about their thoughts about the job, including questions about what Kelsey believed her part should be in all of it.

She looked at the person speaking. "I'll support Wil anyway I can because this is that important to him, and I know he'll always make the right decision to make this area better for everyone."

"Impressive," a gal said, coming behind her. She turned to Wil and gestured toward Kelsey. "Can I borrow your date?" Will nodded. "I'll grab us some drinks."

"Thanks, sweetheart."

~

Once Wil left, Kelsey turned to the lady. "And you are?"

"The governor's wife. My husband is the same guy who laughed at your boyfriend in the buffet line yesterday when you two mentioned politics."

Kelsey blushed. "How embarrassing! Wil thought he was a politician, and I guess he was right."

"Yes, he was, and my husband was impressed by how he answered a no-win question. I'm also impressed by how you just answered that question because I could see the sincerity in your answer."

Kelsey blew a hair out of her eye. "I believe in Wil, and I always have."

"I can see that. What do you think his chances are of receiving this job?"

She shrugged. "I would have no clue, but I do know if Mr. Kelley or the board wants someone who will fight for this land, Wil will be the one."

"I've heard that about the guy and his treasure-hunting experiences. Very accomplished man."

"Thank you. Now, ma'am, what is this really all about?"

The lady grinned. "Very perceptive woman. I just wanted to know more about the gal who's with possibly the next wildlife biologist in this area."

"It was good talking to you, ma'am. I'm going to join Wil." Kelsey hurried over to him.

"Is everything okay?" he asked.

"I think so. She said she wanted to know more about the gal with you. Does it bother you?"

"If you ask if I'm concerned you'll say something that will harm me, no way."

"I guess that's what I was asking."

He motioned to the band that had just started playing. "How about you and I go out on the dance floor?"

She smiled. "I'd love to."

Chapter 35

Kelsey stared out from behind the bar at work, watching everyone talking and drinking. There was no question she was in love with Wil, and it was the best thing that had happened to her. She knew he also loved her, but the question was—would he take the job in Salmon, Idaho? She hoped he would because it would be a new start for both of them.

Wil had left her the pickup, and she drove home after she got off at six. She walked into the cabin to Wil setting the table. "You didn't have to do this."

"I wanted to," he said, hugging her and kissing her. "How was your day?"

"Wonderful, and tonight will be even better."

Wil continued setting the table. "Dinner is about ready, so if you want to change, go for it."

"I'll be right back." Five minutes later Kelsey came out wearing sweatpants and one of Wil's t-shirts. "I'm famished. What do we have?"

"It's Wil Bolton's first try at shells." He pulled out her chair for her.

"That's sweet," she said.

He then dished out a couple of spoonfuls of pasta shells for each of them, poured some wine, and sat down across from her. "Are you ready?"

Kelsey giggled. "Together?"

"Yep."

They dug into their meal. "Wow, this is good," Kelsey said.

"It is," Wil said, taking a sip of wine.

Kelsey was excited. "What about the job in Idaho?"

Wil sighed. "I haven't heard anymore, but I'm sure I will sooner or later. Your feelings?"

She eyed him. "You should take it if you get the chance. I told you we'd make it work somehow. And by the way, this is a wonderful meal. Thank you."

"After we clean up, how about we sit out on the porch and freeze to death."

She laughed. "A gal can't beat that."

The two snuggled into the blanket Kelsey had bought in Utah, along with a couple of beers. "It isn't as cold snuggling together like this," Kelsey said.

Wil stretched his arms. "It feels good just to relax and enjoy the night. I bought something for you."

"What did you do?" Kelsey asked, turning her head toward him.

Reaching into his pocket, he pulled out a long case. He opened the box, took out a necklace, and attached it around her neck.

Kelsey ran her fingers along it. "This is beautiful! Is it real gold from the Black Hills? I've always wanted something like this."

"Now you have it. Happy birthday."

Her eyes lit up. "You remembered."

"Of course, I did."

She stood up, took his hand, pulled him into the

cabin, and led him to the bed. An hour later, she rolled over and rested her head on his shoulder. "That was a perfect ending to a wonderful evening."

"Can I ask you something?"

She sat up. "Sure."

"I've been thinking about this job in Idaho," Wil said.

"Okay?"

"I have a job with Boris for sure in either Denver or Atlanta, doing what I love to do, but I think it's time to break away from my past and move to a future with you. We've both been through some crazy stuff, and I want us to start over with a clean slate. How do you feel about that?"

She rolled over and kissed him. "That's perfect. I'd hope you would consider something like that. As I drove back from work today, I also thought about starting fresh. Getting away from everything that's happened in our lives. And Idaho is beautiful. I know it's not South Dakota, but it would be our first home together, and we would make it wonderful."

Wil peered into her eyes. "Maybe I'm being naive thinking that we can run away from our past lives."

Kelsey gently held his head in her hands. "I'm not your past, but I am your future, and we'll be just fine."

~

Wil's eyes opened when his cell phone vibrated. He turned it on. "Boris, it's been a while."

"It has. How did your interviews go in Idaho?"

He yawned. "I should know something in a couple of weeks."

"I'm glad you're back because I would like you to fly to Chicago this week to discuss our upcoming treasure hunt.”

The comment peaked Wil’s interest. “Has there been developments?”

“Yes, there are at least a few hunts we’re looking at. One is for Viking artifacts, then there’s another involving the Amazon, and finally one involving the Cambodian-Thai border.”

“Wow, that could be somewhat dangerous.”

“It could be, but we’ll have you talk to the group and decide where we’re heading next. Personally, I’d like to hit all three, but we’ll see. Also, Drexel and Jurgens will be involved.”

“What day are you thinking about?”

“A two-day affair, Friday and Saturday.”

“I’ll make it work.”

“Make what work?” Kelsey said, opening her eyes.

He leaned on his elbow. “Boris Loe wants me to fly back to Chicago later this week to discuss the next treasure hunt. I thought you’d like to join me.”

She sat up. “I can’t get up and leave my job just like that.”

He lifted her up into her arms and kissed her. She returned the kiss and stopped to catch her breath. “You’ve persuaded me.”

Chapter 36

The next day, Wil and Kelsey drove to the Lawrence County Sheriff's Department for an update on what was happening with her family. They found two seats in the corner of the waiting room.

"You don't seem to be too nervous about all of this," Wil said.

Kelsey rubbed her thumb over his knuckles. "I am nervous, but I also know no matter what happens, we'll be together, and that's what's important."

He squeezed her hands. "We've really grown a lot since we've been with each other over the past year."

She eyed him. "We have because we've been able to communicate our feelings and thoughts to each other, which is something I never did until you came into my life. You've helped me in so many ways."

Wil searched the room. "You've helped me also. I told you before I couldn't trust you, but I feel I can now, and that's important to me." He shifted in his seat to face her. "I never told you why trust was so important to me. It had to do with my family when I was growing up."

Kelsey squeezed his hand, urging him to continue.

"My father always went back on his word to me.

At the time, I thought it was just me, but it was our whole family that he did that to. I never knew what to expect or what was the truth, and that's where my issue with honesty came from."

She leaned closer to him. "I can understand that, and I guarantee you I will always be honest with you. Thank you for the birthday gift last night." She fingered her necklace. "This is perfect. It was a wonderful evening, but what would have made it better was your chocolate cake."

They both chuckled.

"Wil, Kelsey, please come back." Sheriff Kanter gestured from where he stood behind the counter.

Kelsey flinched. "I was always told when a lawman smiles, it means I'm in trouble."

The sheriff rolled his eyes. "It's not that bad, Kelsey. Come on back."

The three joined the county attorney in the sheriff's office.

The county attorney started the conversation. "First of all, Ms. Lawrence, Eli Grafton has confessed to the killing of Lydia Boone and the guy at Pactola Lake, and he also testified that your father was the one who gave the order. We also verified that with the butler who was let go.

"Grafton's testimony saved him from the death penalty and an expensive court battle. Your father has been arrested and is waiting to be indicted in Chicago at this moment on several charges including murder and drug and diamond trafficking. It'll be a long time before he gets out of prison—all because of your testimony, Ms. Lawrence."

The sheriff turned to the county attorney. "Is

everything wrapped up with this situation?"

"It is here," the county attorney said. "Ms. Lawrence, you're free to go."

Mixed feelings vied for dominance inside her. Her father was in prison. Justice had been served, and she was exonerated. Still, something gnawed at her. Wil hugged her. As they prepared to leave, the sheriff's voice sounded.

"Hold it you two. Don't leave yet. We're not finished."

They turned at the knock on the door. Carlton Hampton, the forest manager of the Black Hills, and Dr. Wyatt entered. "Sorry we're late."

They glanced at each other and returned to their seats. Hampton took over the meeting and introduced the officials from Wyoming, Colorado, Montana, and South Dakota. "To get to the heart of the matter, cattle are being killed in all four of these states, and they all have two things in common — the cows are fed heavy growth hormones and are all being bred from one location. We believe the location is in the Bighorn Mountains in Wyoming."

The sheriff asked how Hampton would know that.

"Each animal that has been killed has a tag that comes from a ranch in that area of Wyoming owned by the Bolton family—yes, a relation to Wil, but for sure he has nothing to do with it, and we're not even sure this group is doing anything illegal, but it's a place to start."

Wil blew out a deep breath. "Since they are my family, you're hoping I'll talk to them?"

Sheriff Kanter nodded. "Wil, Wyoming law enforcement officials are the only authorities who can go in there because of jurisdiction."

"What about federal officials?"

Hampton nodded over at one of the guys sitting next to an older lady. "This is FBI Agent Douglas Franklin, who has been chasing down these culprits for several months. You and Ms. Lawrence will work directly with him on this case along with the Wyoming officials."

Agent Franklin took over the conversation. "Wil, we know that you haven't had a relationship with your family for several years, but we believe that you give us the best chance to get in there to talk to them. Once you do, we'll take over from there."

Wil's eyes darted from one man to another and finally back to the FBI agent. "You realize they may just as well shoot me as let me on their land. Then if I do get in there, how will we know what is happening?"

Agent Franklin sighed. "Good question. Dr. Wyatt has mentioned, along with others, that you would have a unique insight into situations and could quickly grasp if the cows were being drugged or not."

Wil took a deep breath. "I'm not an FBI agent by any means, so I don't know how I could be of any help."

Agent Franklin grinned. "But you have a knack for thinking on your feet and getting in and out of situations."

Wil laughed. "I'm going in by myself?"

"No, Kelsey will join you as your wife, and more importantly, Wil, in your travels you've seen the need in countries for beef, which we hope will reel them in. You have one ally—your grandmother who lives on the ranch. Perhaps you can rekindle that relationship with her. We'll always be near you—only a text away."

Wil rolled his eyes. "That's comforting."

Chapter 37

That afternoon, Wil and Kelsey packed their bags and joined Agent Franklin for a trip to the Wyoming Bighorn Mountains.

As Agent Franklin started the engine, he turned to Wil. "When was the last time you saw your grandparents?"

Wil thought. "Wow, it's been probably five years or more. We weren't the closest of families."

"May I ask what happened?"

Wil rolled down his window a crack. "Simple, I didn't agree with what my parents and grandparents were doing."

Agent Franklin put on his blinker to turn. "I read their file about how they escaped from the East Coast, faking their death in a car wreck. I also investigated the Lydia Boone situation a few years ago. There's no question that your family knew exactly what was happening, but we could never pin anything on them."

"How long have you been chasing my family?"

Agent Franklin rubbed his chin. "For more than five years. They are very slippery, but all criminals will make a mistake, and we'll be there to nab them."

Wil stared out the window at the Black Hills.

"Agent Franklin, my family is evil at the core and will never go in peacefully. A whole lot of people could get hurt before they turn themselves in."

"We realize that."

They arrived in Buffalo, Wyoming, around nightfall. The agent dropped the "newlyweds" off at a local hotel. "This is where we cut ties from now on. Your family is in an area near Burgess Junction and the Medicine Wheel Passage. You're already registered for a room. Here are the keys to a Range Rover you'll need when the roads get bad. And here is a burner phone you will use to contact us if needed. I need to take your cell phone until everything is finished. Good luck."

"Yeah, thanks," Wil said, as he handed Agent Franklin their cell phones.

Kelsey linked her arm with Wil's, and they headed into the hotel to the front desk.

Wil smiled at the redhead behind the desk. "A room reservation for Wil Bolton."

The desk clerk looked through her list. "Welcome, Mr. and Mrs. Bolton. Here is your room key and complimentary breakfast tickets in the morning."

"Do you know anything about the Bighorn Mountains?"

The desk clerk was excited. "Oh yes, sir, it is a popular tourist attraction, and people love to hunt and fish up there. Are you planning on doing any of that?"

"We want to see it because people have told us how beautiful it is."

"Oh yes, it is beautiful. One place you won't want to miss is the Cloud Peak Wilderness Area. Very few people live out there, but there are a couple of major cattle ranches in that area." The lady realized who Wil was. "In fact, one of the family's there is the Boltons. Are they related to you?"

His ears perked up. "How do you know them?"

She grinned. "My sister is married to Del. They have a couple of children and are expecting a third soon."

"Now that I know they're up there, I hope to see them."

The next morning Wil and Kelsey climbed into the Range Rover. Kelsey slid over next to Wil and kissed him on the cheek. "I'm going to enjoy this."

Wil rolled his eyes. "I can tell."

She rolled the ring on her finger and grinned. "This isn't necessarily the wedding ring I would have chosen, but it'll do until you put a real one on my finger."

They traveled for thirty minutes before Kelsey pointed toward the mountains. Her eyes watched the wild animals. "Look at that herd of elk making their way out of the mountains on that trail."

Wil pulled over to the side to take some photos. "That is so cool."

The two stepped out and shot some photos. Kelsey peered up at Wil. "I read that people usually don't see so many elk out here. They're more likely to live deep in the mountains. The elk must realize the hunting season is over. Have you ever hunted?"

Wil took another photo. "When I was young. I'm not an avid hunter, but I know people who love to hunt. As you know, I'm a guide in the Black Hills for hunters."

Kelsey surveyed her map. "We need to take Middle Creek Road, and from what I can tell, it doesn't look too accessible, especially during the winter."

They turned onto the road and hit a couple of bumps.

She pointed to the right. "Take that road."

"Sawmill Creek Road?"

They had traveled up the gravel road about five miles when they ran into two guards standing at a gate. One slipped through the slight opening in the gates while the other kept his rifle pointed at Wil.

Kelsey took a deep breath. "Maybe this wasn't such a good idea."

"Too late to turn back." Wil lowered his window as the security guard came over to him.

"This is private property, and no one is allowed without prior authority."

Wil smiled. "I think my grandparents would be unhappy if you didn't let me through to see them."

"You're saying you're a Bolton?"

"I am Wil, and this is my wife, Kelsey. We're visiting Wyoming and understand my grandparents live in this area, and we'd like to say 'hi' to them."

The security guard laughed. "Yeah, right. From what I understand, your grandparents want nothing to do with you."

Wil took a deep breath. "Let them decide."

The security guard's eyes narrowed. "I'll be right back."

Once he left, Kelsey squeezed Wil's hand hard. "Calm down, you've been able to hold your composure in the past, and I know you can do it now."

The guard came back five minutes later smiling. "You're in luck, Your grandfather was very interested in seeing you before—" He laughed. "Drive through about two miles, and you'll see the house over the hill.

We may see you again, or we may not."

Once they drove through, Kelsey turned to Wil. "What did he mean by that?"

"My grandfather has no liking for me." Wil drove for a half a mile. "Wow, this is huge." Cattle dotted the landscape as far as their eyes could see.

It was ten minutes later when Wil and Kelsey came to a large ranch house. Several guards stood at strategic locations.

Wil stopped the pickup, and one of the guards came up to the window to check him over. The house's door opened and out came a large guy with blond hair and a beard.

Wil leapt out of the car when he saw his older brother Del.

He strode over. "Wil, what the hell are you doing here?"

"I was in the area, and I heard my family was around, so I thought I'd stop in to say hi."

Del laughed. "Not likely." He stared at Kelsey and then back to Wil. "You and Kelsey finally decided to get hitched?"

"We're hoping to start a family soon."

Del grinned. "She looks like she'll be a good candidate for many children." He turned back to Wil. "Grandma would be glad to see you, but you're not welcome up here by anyone else."

Wil and Kelsey climbed out of the car and walked toward the door of the house. Kelsey reached over and grabbed his hand. Del stepped back as they walked in, followed by Wil. Del touched his shoulder and whispered to him. "One wrong move, and I'll gladly put a bullet in your head."

Chapter 38

Grandma Bolton looked up at Wil when he walked in, a tear trailing from her eye. "Wil, it's been so long. Where have you been? Come here and let me see you?"

He walked over to her, and she wrapped her frail arms around his waist. "I'm so happy you're here. We were just sitting down for lunch—mountain stew soup, a specific recipe I came up with since we moved up here. Will you join us?" She turned to Kelsey. "You're the one who stole my grandson's heart?"

Kelsey smiled. "It wasn't too hard. His beautiful blue eyes attracted me to him and haven't let go."

They turned to an older man with long white hair and a beard. He walked with a cane. "Where did you meet him?"

Kelsey eyed the old man. "You must be his grandfather?"

He stared at her. "How did you meet him?"

She pushed the hair out of her eyes. "On a cobblestone street in Deadwood."

When Wil's grandfather's head tilted at Kelsey response, Wil jumped in. "Grandpa, I'd think you'd be happy to see me, but I guess not."

He growled. "You would be right, Wil. As far as I'm concerned, I wished my son's wife hadn't given birth to you."

Grandma Bolton jumped in. "Dear, that's enough. He's your grandson, so calm down," Grandma Bolton said. "Let's eat lunch."

During lunch Kelsey put down her spoon. "We saw a lot of cattle out there in the mountains. Are they yours?"

"They are," Grandpa Bolton said.

Kelsey continued. "Did you know that Wil has met cattle experts in his travels that have told him things about their cattle situation?"

Grandpa Bolton's eyes lifted up. "Is that so? What do you know about cattle? From what I understand all you do is chase down treasures."

"People in other countries have to eat also," Wil said.

It drew a laugh from several members around the table until Grandpa Bolton squelched it with a glare. Wil could tell everyone was afraid of him. "We all know about how much beef Japan, China, and South Korea buy, but did you know that the Philippines and Vietnam are in the market for more American beef? I found that out on one of my treasure hunts in the South Pacific."

His grandfather's face changed to one of interest.

Wil continued. "Like Kelsey said, while I don't have a direct connection with those in power in those countries, I do have connections with those who work with them at times."

"Is that so?" Grandpa Bolton said. "Who?"

Wil grinned. "Grandpa, you just told me I don't

belong here, and Del has said the same thing. Why would I give you any information after Del threatened my life?"

Grandpa Bolton laughed for the first time. "You are so much different than any other person in our family. You actually have some guts."

~

After lunch, as Wil and Kelsey walked outside, Kelsey quickly grabbed his hand. "They scare me. The only reason you're not dead is because your grandmother cares about you."

Wil sighed. "That's what I hoped." They were standing near a tree when Wil took Kelsey into his arms, kissed her, and she responded in kind.

"Isn't that sweet out in public Wil Bolton kissing a gal."

Wil kept his same expression. "What do you want, Del?"

"Grandpa wants to show you something. I told him no, but he insisted on it, so come with me. Mrs. Bolton, my wife would like to talk to you."

Del and Wil walked toward a large barn. Inside was Grandpa Bolton and several men feeding calves. "Wil, I'd like to show you what we do here, so you can pass it on to your contacts. Maybe they'll think of dealing with us directly."

Wil didn't say anything but followed him through the large barn with a guard beside him at all times.

His grandfather pointed toward a stall. "We're not even close to the largest cattle operations in China and Australia, whose cattlemen own in the millions of acres, but we have thirty-thousand acres here, and this barn is a ten-thousand-foot facility that holds several thousand cows at one time, which is fairly large in this region of the country."

Wil peered at his grandfather. "What are they feeding the cattle?"

He looked at his grandson. "Typically, we feed alfalfa hay and grass hay, along with corn, barley, and wheat, which at times can be expensive because of the terrain we live in. It means we have to bring a lot of food in."

"I'm sure that would be costly."

"It is, but when we sell our cattle, it more than makes up for it."

While his grandfather turned to talk to his guard, Wil poured a handful of feed into a small Ziplock bag he had brought along and stuffed it into his pocket. Just then he saw a mounted camera, so turned his back on the camera before he grabbed a handful of another type of feed.

Wil pointed to the camera as his grandfather turned back to him. "A lot of surveillance, I see?"

The old man smiled. "Oh yes, we're totally prepared for any situation." His grandfather spent almost an hour in the barn and out with the cattle, extolling the wonders of his cattle ranch. Once they were finished, the group sat outside of the barn on a table with benches.

He leaned against a wall. "Wil, do you have any questions?"

"No, it's pretty straightforward. Based on our past relationships it's hard to believe you'd even show me or talk to me about any of this stuff."

His grandfather stared at him. "We aren't doing anything illegal here, and if there is any way you can help us make more money, it's worth it."

Wil took a deep breath. "In the Black Hills, there have been a couple of cows shot by rifles and left for dead. Have you had those problems up here?"

The comment didn't move his grandfather. "There are always those concerns, as there are with coyotes and mountain lions who take out cattle here or there. It's part of the business."

A large truck pulled in. His grandfather stood. "I'd talk more, but I have business clients to talk to. Hopefully, this will help you explain to your contacts what we're doing up here. Please escort him and his wife off the premises, Del?"

"Yes, sir."

Wil and Del walked toward the house when Kelsey hurried over to him and hugged him. "Did you get the grand tour?"

"We did," he said, slipping the bag of feed between her breasts. She didn't change her expression. Wil spoke once more, "We've overstayed our welcome."

Kelsey grinned. "Then I guess it's time we leave."

They turned at Del's voice. "Hold it, Wil, we have to check you before you leave the premises."

Wil rolled his eyes. "You've had me under surveillance since I walked into this place."

Del grinned. "Then you have nothing to worry about."

The guard came over to Wil. "Let's do it."

Wil lifted his arms and spread his legs a bit. The guard checked him thoroughly and then turned to Del. "Nothing."

"Okay, little brother, you're free to go. One thing, if you try to harm our grandparents, I'll make sure those closest to you receive the same fate."

Wil eyed Del. "Nothing has changed."

As they drove back toward the gate, Kelsey slid over next to him and squeezed his hand. "I was scared the whole time."

Wil smirked. "You were great back there."

Chapter 39

The two drove back to the hotel, switched into bathing suits, and took the elevator down to the hot tub to soak and talk about what they'd just been through. Once they were both in the hot tub, Kelsey slid near him so they could talk in private.

"Del's wife wants to escape, Wil. She's been beaten several times by Del, and she's scared and doesn't know what to do."

Wil took a deep breath. "Another layer to add to the story. Maybe when we talk to Douglas, he can figure out a way to rescue her."

Kelsey moved onto his lap and gazed at him. "As scared as I was, I'm glad that I'm here with you." She kissed him gently on the lips. "That's for being there today to help me with my fears."

"You did just fine out there. What happens tomorrow will determine everything."

Once they got out of the hot tub and dried off, they made their way up to the room. Wil picked up the burner phone and called Douglas. He put it on the speaker phone.

"Wil, I've been waiting to hear from you. What have you found out?"

Wil thought about what he wanted to say. "Good and bad. Good is that my brother didn't put a bullet in my head, and bad is the fact they're watching every move I make. I've seen a guy tracking me since I left the ranch."

"You did find the ranch?"

"Yeah, they're way up in the mountains, which makes it hard to get to them, and they have guards everywhere. To make matters worse, Del's wife wants out and may turn evidence if we get her out of there."

The could hear the excitement in the agent's voice. "Are you sure of that?"

Kelsey interrupted. "I talked to her, Agent Douglas, and she is scared, has been physically abused by Del, and will run when she gets a chance. She won't get too far, but she's going to try."

"Anything else?"

Wil jumped in. "I have a bag full of grain they feed the cows for you guys to analyze. I'll put it in our box for room 225. You can pick it up there. It'll be wrapped in a fancy package with a bow."

Douglas laughed once more. "Merry Christmas. This I have to see. What is the play?"

"My grandfather showed me around the place today because I told him I knew some big players around the world. He seems interested, so if you could line up a couple of cattle buyers from Vietnam and the Philippines, we may have a chance. I told him they are hurting for cattle, which they probably are."

"We'll set something up in the next day or two. Once I find the buyers, I'll contact you, and then we'll work to get them into the ranch. Also, another cow was killed not too far from the Bolton ranch with the same caliber bullet."

Wil took a deep breath. "Did you think my family might be involved?"

"Everything points to them, but who knows?"

Wil ended the conversation. "Tomorrow we'll try to find a back way into the ranch."

~

Wil and Kelsey pulled on to U.S. 14 toward the Bighorn Mountains. "The snow is still heavy in the higher elevations," Wil said. After an hour of driving, they reached Cloud Peak Wilderness, but instead of going toward the entrance to Wil's grandparents ranch, they deviated more to the west under Kelsey's direction. "Stop here."

Wil did that.

She opened the door. "Join me"

The two jumped out of the truck, Kelsey grabbed his hand, and walked over to a peak overlooking an open area.

"Beautiful," Wil said. "How did you know about this?"

She continued staring at the view. "I did some googling and found a couple talking on YouTube about their different experiences. One of the places was this one, so I sent them a message about it, and they gave me the exact directions. I'm not only doing it for romantic purposes—if you look to the northeast, you may notice something."

Wil glanced that way. "I assume it's my grandparents' ranch?"

For the next hour they enjoyed the scenery. Wil pointed to an eagle flying over the horizon.

Kelsey turned to what he was looking at.

"Beautiful."

She pointed at something. "I can't make that out. Are those people?"

Wil hustled back to the pickup and grabbed a set of binoculars. "It looks like two guys. They're tracking something or someone."

Kelsey was worried. "Can we do anything to help the person they're tracking?"

Wil quickly searched the area. "I see two children." Wil did a double take. "My eyes are seeing something I can't believe. It looks like a woman with two children."

"Is it Del's wife?"

"That would be my guess. Okay, I may be able to reach her before the trackers do. Drive the truck toward that location."

She squeezed his hand. "Stay safe."

Wil took a deep breath. "I'll do my best."

~

Wil raced in the direction he thought she was heading. In his mind, the gal was just trying to get away and at this point didn't care what happened. He jumped ahead of her, and as she came up a path, he grabbed her and covered her mouth with his hand. The two children stared up scared to do anything.

She struggled until she saw who it was.

"I got you. We have to reach the truck." He pointed.

She looked dismayed holding on to her two children. "How did you know? No matter, thank you, my name is Meredith, and these are my two children, and as you can tell, a third one is coming."

"We'll talk later. Just hurry to the truck."

She nodded and headed in the direction Wil had

pointed. Wil watched for a minute as she hurried away. Once he saw she was going in the right direction, he turned back to the trackers. They were within hearing distance.

Wil heard a voice. "How the hell can a lady with two children escape us?"

Then a different voice. "She's been planning this for a long time."

The first person spoke again. "If we don't find her, we probably should think about escaping also. Let's split up. You go to the southwest, I'll go northwest, and we should be able to circle around to catch her."

Wil watched as the two went in different directions. His first target would be the guy to the northwest because he would be closer to the pickup. He crept alongside him, keeping behind the tree line. Wil beat the tracker to the location among a group of trees and waited for him. When the guy walked past, Wil grabbed him from behind, knocking him out before he could see who it was, and grabbed the rifle he was carrying.

Wil searched for the other tracker but didn't see him. Just as he saw Del's wife approach the pickup with her children, he heard a shot. No! Wil raced toward them as another shot was fired, but it missed its mark. The guy must be too far away. The lady jumped into the pickup with her kids. Kelsey backed up and took off, leaving Wil to fend for himself. He was okay with that because now they were safe, at least for the time being.

One big problem was the man would recognize Wil's pickup and blow everything. Wil didn't want to kill the guy, but it might need to happen. He hurried over to where the man was and shot at the ground in front of him.

The guy whipped around ready to fire. "Don't try it. I can plug you right where you stand."

The guy snickered. "Del was right. You're coming after the Boltons, but the problem is you don't have anything because the family is doing everything legal with the cattle."

Wil kept his eyes alert. "Maybe the cattle are legal, but he's holding a gal against her will, and that's kidnapping—a felony in the United States."

The man laughed. "This is Wyoming, mister."

Wil couldn't believe what the guy just said. "The last thing I heard, Wyoming was still in the United States. Now drop the rifle."

The man did as he was told.

"Kick it away from you. Okay, we have a long walk, but there's something I have to do before we start." Wil reached into his backpack and took out some rope. He tied the man's hands to the front of him and then started to gag him when he started talking.

"You realize there are others looking for that woman and her children."

Wil pushed him along. "Then you had better hope we don't run into them."

Chapter 40

"What is going on?" Kelsey asked, as she drove away with the woman and her children.

Crying, Del's wife said, "I planned to escape as soon as I could, and everything lined up today. I'm sorry your husband is dead."

Kelsey shook her head. "No, he went after the other two so we could escape. We'll head back to Buffalo as soon as I make this call." Kelsey moved away from her and called the number Wil had given her.

"Wil, is that you?" a gruff voice said on the other end.

"No, this is Kelsey."

"Mrs. Bolton, what are you doing on this phone?"

"Del Bolton's wife has escaped, and I have her right now. Wil is chasing two trackers down in the Cloud Peak Wilderness area. Save him and Del's wife and kids."

"Can you give me the coordinates?"

She tried to remember what Wil had said about finding the coordinates, then selected an app and landed on the right site. "I can meet you at a small cabin about three miles from here. Here are the coordinates. Please hurry!"

"We'll be there."

"Sir, he's in trouble."

~

Wil continued along a trail with the man gagged and tied. Every once in a while, Wil would turn to make sure no one was following. The man stopped when he did, and Wil could read the warning in his angry eyes. "You'd better hope they don't find us because I won't regret killing anyone who keeps a person against their will."

This time the man's eyes took on a glint of fear.

"Let's move."

The man continued on. "You don't even want to know my name?"

"Nope, I just know that you were hunting a gal and her two children for my brothers and have a deep scar on your face."

"Yeah, Del did that because he didn't like the way I looked at his wife. By the way my name is Ernest Simpson."

The two traveled for another two hours before Wil found a place they could rest with good cover. He reached into his backpack and put a protein bar in the tied hands of the man. He untied the guy's gag. "I need you to keep up your strength because I sure the hell don't want to drag you, but I will if I have to."

The man laughed as he chewed on the protein bar. "You have no clue what you've gotten yourself into. There is so much going on up here that you have no idea about."

Wil slowly chewed his bar. "I'm sure you'll be talking to the authorities when we catch up with them."

The guy was spooked. "Never. Your two brothers will kill me before I get a chance. You've signed both our death warrants. If you would have taken Del's wife, we would have just disappeared. Del would have never let us live."

Wil handed him some water and the man thirstily drank. He handed it back to Wil. Wil took a drink himself. "I know somethings going on here but not sure, but will figure it out."

The guy sighed. "You know a lot more than you should, but the problem for you is pinning them on any of us."

"Don't be too sure. I'm sure you'll be a key witness, as will Del's wife."

"Del's wife will never spill the beans on anything because she knows Del will find her, kill her, her dad, sister, and children. She won't ever let that happen."

Wil pushed him on. "We'll have to see."

The two continued on down the trail. Wil hadn't put the gag back on the man because of the high altitude.

Ernest stopped and glared at Wil. "Do you even know where you're going?"

Wil surveyed the area. "Yep, someplace your boss wouldn't expect."

"And how would you know where to go? You've never been out here."

Wil grinned. "Simple, it's called a map. Let's keep moving. We still have plenty of daylight to find a place to stay."

Ernest laughed. "Del is right. You are one crazy dude."

~

Kelsey paced beside the truck. The guy she called hadn't shown up yet, and it had been thirty minutes.

Minutes later a vehicle came into view—actually, three vehicles. She turned to Meredith. "Do you know them?"

She shook her head.

Kelsey climbed out of the pickup and waited as a tall guy in a black suit and tie stepped out one of the Range Rovers.

Agent Franklin hurried to them. "I'm sorry it took so long."

"You're here, and that's all that matters."

The thin man nodded toward Meredith. "Let's get you and your children to safety, Ms. Bolton."

"My dad, sister, and brother also," Del's wife said. "They'll be after them."

The agent sighed. "We already taken care of them. They're safe."

He turned to Kelsey. "Are you ready?"

She shook her head. "Thank you, but sir, I'm not leaving without Wil."

Agent Franklin's eyes widened. "You have no idea where he is?"

"He'll head to Sheridan, and I'll be there waiting for him."

He smiled. "Okay then, I'll send someone with you to help you."

Kelsey took a deep breath. "Please, I have to do this myself."

He emitted a sigh. "Here's another burner phone. Have him call me and use this code, 'Chopper Crew.'"

Chapter 41

The sun was setting as Wil and his prisoner made their way down a trail in the mountains. His hope was to reach the main road before it got too dark and find a place to call the local sheriff's department. He finally found the main road.

Ernest peered at Wil. "I'll be damned."

Wil grinned. "Road maps help a lot."

They traveled for another forty minutes as cars whizzed by. Wil had just about given up hope that anyone would give them a ride when a heavy blue pickup truck stopped in front of them.

The driver jumped out, ran over to Wil, and kissed him hard on the lips. Kelsey let out her breath. "You're okay?"

Wil was shocked. "How did you find us?"

"I just thought like you did, which is pretty scary because here you are." She turned to the guy Wil held by the arm. "What happened to your partner?"

Ernest dropped his eyes to the ground. "He's probably dead by now, if not, he'll wished for death when the boss hears."

Wil jerked the guy forward. "Let's get him into the back of the truck. You drive, honey."

"Can I talk to you for a minute?" Kelsey asked.

Wil tied Simpson to the side of the truck and walked over to where Kelsey stood.

Kelsey pulled on his arm. "You're supposed to call Agent Douglas with this burner phone and give him the code, 'Chopper Crew.'"

"Okay, here's what we're going to do. You'll drive us to the rendezvous Agent Douglas has set up, and I'll make sure he doesn't jump out the back."

"That's it?"

"That's it. Let's do it. And thank you for coming back for me."

She smiled. "I wasn't going to let anything happen to my 'husband.'"

~

Kelsey hopped into the truck, and once the other two were in back, she drove toward their destination, Big Horn. She tried to control her emotions, but her hands trembled. Would Wil's grandfather's lackeys ambush them along the way?

They arrived in Big Horn an hour later and drove toward a renovated hotel. Hopefully, this was where the FBI would be waiting for them. Google Maps showed they were only nine miles from Sheridan and fourteen miles to the Montana border.

Wil grabbed Simpson out of the back of the vehicle and waited for Kelsey to join him. "Are you okay?"

She tried to calm herself down. "I'm scared."

Simpson laughed. "You should be because you've just signed a death warrant for your family."

Wil sighed. "I'd worry about what's going to happen to you if I were you. I've heard about these Black Ops sites that the FBI, CIA, and other covert operations used to convince people to talk. I'm sure it won't be long before you spill your guts."

Simpson growled and Wil took him into the hotel. Waiting for them were Kelsey, Del's wife, her two children—a young girl, a young boy—and an older man standing with Douglas.

Kelsey approached Meredith and hugged her. "Are you okay?"

She sighed. "The guy scared me to death when he showed up and grabbed us. I thought he was another one of Del's hatchet men, like Simpson."

Kelsey nodded her head toward Wil who had delivered Simpson to the agent, then turned back to Meredith. "I'm happy Wil found you."

Meredith's father spoke up. "We're waiting for the agent to decide what's going to happen. He's been mum about everything so far. There's been a lot of chatter in the corner over there—or the command center, as one of the guys called it."

Kelsey laughed. "Always so dramatic, these government officials. You sound like you're loving it."

"I'm relieved to have my family back."

Kelsey searched for Wil and saw him talking to Douglas. "Excuse me, I need to talk to my husband."

Del's wife smiled. "You're fortunate to land a man like that."

Kelsey smiled. "I agree." She joined Wil who was waiting for Douglas to finish what he was doing with Simpson. He touched her face. "Everything okay?"

She took his hand and pulled him away from the others. "What is going to happen with them?"

Wil put his arm around her. "It depends on what Del's wife says. If she testifies against her husband, then they'll all be put into witness protection."

She peered into his eyes. "And if she doesn't?"

He squeezed her shoulders. "To be truthful, I can't believe there's a scenario where she wouldn't do that; especially since she tried to escape from them."

"Wil, she knows nothing about what's happening there. She ran because she's tired of getting beaten by your brother."

Wil took a deep breath. "That's a whole different scenario then. That would all be up to Agent Douglas and how he wants to handle it, maybe even finding relatives elsewhere."

Agent Douglas heard the last comment. "It would suck, but Wil has come up with something that will help. I need to talk to him for a minute alone."

~

Wil joined Agent Douglas for a walk to another part of the building. Once they arrived, Douglas studied the area, then gestured to a quiet corner. "I'm surprised that Mrs. Bolton was able to escape from her husband. She knows nothing to help us nail your family because she knows nothing about the operation. I have a judge who is issuing a restraining order against Del Bolton, but from what you've said, that probably wouldn't do any good."

Wil thought. "Does the family have relatives anywhere else in the area?"

Agent Douglas nodded. "From what their father said, they have an older son who lives in Seattle, Washington, but they don't have the money to fly there."

Wil searched for the family. "If I can talk them into it, I'll pay for their flight."

"You'd do that?"

"Anything to get them away from my family."

"Okay, I'll make arrangements to fly them there. By the way, the samples already came back, and they tested positive for an illegal steroid in the feed that helps with growth of the cattle, so you were right. In addition, I found a buyer from the Philippines who is interested in checking out their cattle. He'll be contacting them tomorrow. The company owner is actually legitimate and very thorough. He will figure out what's happening with the cattle no matter what your family tries. Of course, you and your wife will have to broker the deal."

Wil groaned. "If Simpson finds a way to escape, we'll both be dead. You realize that."

Agent Franklin grinned. "Then we'll have to make sure he doesn't escape."

Wil returned to the building entrance to where Kelsey waited for her, took her hand, and the two walked outside.

"Are you okay?" she asked.

"I'm fine. The packet of feed we brought back is contaminated with some kind of illegal hormones, and we have a legitimate buyer who will go in tomorrow to talk to my family about purchasing cattle. He will be very thorough and will find out that the cows aren't what they're supposed to be."

Kelsey took his hand. "Does this buyer even know what's going on?"

"Nope, which is good. The feds will bust them right there. The problem is in order to complete this deal, you and I will have to broker it. And Douglas is going to fly the family to Washington."

She smiled. "Oh my, according to Meredith, they've been wanting to go there for the longest time, but they've never had the money. Hold it, they still don't have the money, and we both know the government won't pay for anything like that." When he didn't answer, Kelsey peered into Wil's eyes. "You're paying for it." She reached over and planted a solid kiss on his lips, then stepped back and tried to catch her breath. "Wow, I'd like to do that again."

Chapter 42

The next morning Wil contacted his grandfather and told him about the meeting later that afternoon with the contingent from the Philippines. It was set for two at the ranch. He turned as Kelsey and Agent Douglas joined him. "It's all set," Wil said.

Wil turned to the others. "Great. The family is in Seattle, and it sounds like their brother is excited to have them there, and they plan on staying there, from what Del's wife said."

Agent Douglas took over the conversation. "Wil, these buyers have no idea you two are working for us, so it's important to keep it that way. Just connect them with your family and get out of there."

Wil shook his head. "That's not how my grandfather operates. We can't go anywhere until he believes everything is cool."

Agent Franklin had a worried face. "That brings up a problem. I can't send you two in without sufficient backup. You won't come out alive."

Wil grinned at Douglas. "I can handle things. This is my chance to put the family behind bars; something that should have happened many years ago."

Douglas's jaw tightened. "It's against my better

judgment, but let's do this."

Wil and Kelsey drove to Sheridan to meet the group from the Philippines. There were a dozen in the contingent; Wil noticed at least four security guards. There was also an interpreter who Wil spoke to.

"Welcome to America," Wil said.

The head of the contingent stared at Kelsey. "And who is this?"

He introduced Kelsey. "My wife helped me broker this deal with you. It's important that she's with us because the family is very particular in how they do business, and she was in on the first meeting."

"Understood," the interpreter said.

The interpreter and the two main guys in the group joined Wil and Kelsey in the cab pickup. Kelsey slid in next to Wil with the interpreter on the passenger side. The other nine followed in two other king-cab trucks.

The interpreter smiled. "They're excited about riding in a king-cab truck."

Wil took a deep breath. "We'll need it where we're going."

The interpreter relayed the message. They started the drive up the mountain to the Cloud Peak Wilderness area. Kelsey tapped Wil on the arm. "Over there."

Wil peeked to the north and saw an elk going through the pass. He stopped the truck and turned to the interpreter. "Elk. They may want photos."

The interpreter passed it onto the two in back and they nodded. For the next ten minutes the passengers in the three vehicles continued to snap photos. Wil went to the interpreters. "We should get going."

They traveled another twenty minutes before they reached the front gate of the Bolton Ranch. The security guard checked all three vehicles before waving them through. Waiting at the ranch house were Grandpa Bolton, Del, and Cole.

"Crap."

Kelsey turned to Wil quickly. "What?"

Wil tilted his head to what he saw. "Cole is there."

Kelsey frowned. "That could be bad."

"We'll find out." Wil climbed out of the truck and helped Kelsey out. The others joined them. His grandfather introduced himself and the group with him, as did the interpreter with the others.

"I'm glad you could make it," Grandpa Bolton said. "We made some treats specifically for you. Please join us."

They walked inside, and the Philippine contingent oohed and aahed at the table setting. Grandma Bolton pressed her hands together. "We will try our best to make you feel at home. First, we have the Filipino adobo with a twist. We used pork belly instead of chicken and added pineapple. We hope you enjoy it."

She moved to another portion of the table. "Here we have vegetarian *pancit*, which you know is a plant-based version of the popular noodle dish, and finally, mini *bicol* express bites, which you know as the spicy coconut-milk dish."

Grandpa Bolton gestured for everyone to sit down. "Please join us." He walked over to Wil and Kelsey. "You did your job, grandson. Would you two know what happened to Del's wife?"

"What *happened* to her?" Wil asked, adopting a puzzled expression.

Grandpa Bolton studied the two of them, then offered a thin smile. "You either know nothing about her leaving, or you're a very cool customer, and so is your wife."

Kelsey took Wil's hand then whispered in his ear. "Let's go mingle, sweetheart. Right now, we need to stay focused, so we can get out of here alive."

He winked at her. "Are you sure you aren't an undercover agent?"

She rolled her eyes. "Not even close. I'm scared to death here that we won't get out of this alive."

Wil wrapped his arm around her shoulder. "So far, so good."

Del walked over to join the two. "We're ready to give our guests a tour, and the interpreter said the bosses want you along to make sure everything runs smoothly. It had better."

Wil took a deep breath. The leader of the group stayed near Wil with the interpreter by his side. Grandpa Bolton showed him everything in the barn including how the calves and cattle were taken care of.

The leader said something to the interpreter who then turned to Grandpa Bolton. "I'd like to examine what you feed the cattle."

Grandpa Bolton smiled. "The normal things—oats, hay, and other grains."

The interpreter relayed it to the leader, who then looked over at Wil. Kelsey whispered to him. "He's putting you on the spot."

Wil asked the interpreter what he wanted to know. The interpreter explained that the boss wanted to test the feed ingredients.

Del jumped in right away. "That would be difficult because that would take time."

The leader shook his head at his interpreter's

words. "What's going on?" Grandpa Bolton asked.

The interpreter repeated the leader's request. "He wants to check different feed products before he makes a final decision, and he wants Wil Bolton to choose the feed."

Cole who was standing behind Wil whispered in his ear. "Tread lightly."

Wil grabbed a handful of grain from the nearest of five bins and handed it to the interpreter, then did the same for two other bins. As he went to grab a handful from a fourth bin, Cole slapped it out of Wil's hand. "I'm so sorry," he said.

The interpreter turned to the leader who spewed out a slew of words, and then turned back to Grandpa Bolton. "He wishes to check *that* bag of feed."

Wil could sense the tension building. Grandpa Bolton took a deep breath. "I'm sorry. That was an accident. We will grab you more out of that bag."

His grandfather reached down ostensibly to grab some feed from the fourth bin, but Wil saw him take it from a bag underneath. The leader must have caught it also because he barked an order.

"What the hell is going on?" Grandpa Bolton asked.

The leader spoke in English. "We have all the evidence we need. Arrest all of them for illegal hormones in their feed."

"Damn you, Wil," Del went for his neck. The interpreter blocked him. As Del whipped around to leave, the FBI agents barged through the door blocking Del's escape.

"Take them away," Agent Douglas said.

Chapter 43

The interrogations began in Big Horn. The FBI took Wil and Kelsey to a different location.

Agent Douglas joined them after a few minutes. "You should hear them all squawking about what's happening. We have this all under wraps, and your family is going to prison for a long time." He gazed over at Kelsey. "You held your cool like a pro."

She took a deep breath. "I noticed Wil's expression didn't change, so I tried to imitate him hoping this was all a joke."

Agent Franklin sighed. "I couldn't tell you about our plant because it was the only way we could protect you two. Now you can both leave, but if you two are ever interested in helping us out in the future, let me know."

"I don't think so," Kelsey said. "Once is enough."

After Agent Douglas left, Wil and Kelsey walked outside and sat down on a bench.

She took his hand. "That was something I never imagined would happen in my life."

"Then why did you agree to do it?"

She ran a hand over the day's growth of stubble on his cheek. "Because we did it together."

~

It was late June, and the snow had melted in the Black Hills. Over the past month, Wil and Kelsey drew even closer together than they had been before. Wil sat on a bench along Deadwood's Main Street when Kelsey walked out of the souvenir shop with a bag. She set the bag next to him, crawled onto his lap, and wrapped her arms around his neck. "I'm looking for a certain guy because I have some important news to tell him."

He rolled his eyes. "Funny, I'm also looking for a certain gal because I have some major news to tell her. What does this guy look like?"

She touched his face. "Let me think. He has beautiful blue eyes, stands six-one, and rolls his eyes exactly like you just did, which is a bit adorable. When I first met him, he had long light brown hair with a beard, but now he wears it shorter, and the beard is gone."

Wil put his arm around her. "Do you prefer him with the beard or without the beard?"

Kelsey laid her head on his shoulder. "Definitely without the beard because I can touch his smooth face with my hands, and it feels so good. Tell me about the gal you're looking for."

"Let's see, when I first met her, it was on this exact spot, and I heard her laugh for the first time when I told her I was counting cobblestones. She has a beautiful laugh, and the way she blushes is cute. This particular girl wore the same outfit you're wearing right now—a light green strapless mini-skirt with heels, but it seems the heels are three-inch heels versus one-inch she'd worn before."

Kelsey grinned. "Sounds like a sexy gal."

"And what's more," Wil said. "She has the most beautiful sparkling green eyes and light brown hair, that was mid-length at the time, but she did let it grow out longer over the past few months."

She peered up at him. "Which do you prefer?"

"Hm, I like it both ways, but if I had my choice, it would be the mid-length. It was exactly one year ago today that I met this gal for the first time, and over the past year I've fallen deeply in love with her and can't get her out of my mind. In fact—" Wil lifted Kelsey off his lap and sat her on the bench, then peered into her eyes. "I remember telling this gal that once I finally got a job where I could support her, I would ask her to marry me. Well, a year later I have an offer to be a wildlife biologist in Salmon, Idaho, so I'm making good on my promise." He bent down on one knee. "Kelsey Marie Lawrence, will you marry me?"

Kelsey's lips quivered. "I'd hoped the particular guy I was looking for would finally marry me because of the news I had to tell him. Remember when we thought he was going to be a father at Christmas, and we were both crushed when it didn't happen, but Wilton Edgar Bolton, for sure you are going to be a father. I'm pregnant."

Wil lifted her up. "Wow, that is wonderful."

She kissed him. "It's perfect. I always knew this day would come, and it couldn't come at a better place. You're the only guy I've ever loved."

Wil lifted her onto his lap. "You never gave up on us."

Kelsey placed her hands around his head and stared deeply into his eye. "How could I when you're the guy who stole my heart?"

THE END

Other books by this author

Bouncing Back

The Battle Off the Court

Success on the Hard Wood

Tragedy Off the Court

Freedom Flight

Fight for Survival

Road to Hell

A New Life Begins

Relentless

Missing

Targeted

The Reluctant Adventurer

Underwater Passage

Author Bio: My wife, Susan and I have two sons, Justin (Kayla) and Jeremy and a grandson, Aiden. Born and raised in South Dakota. I enjoy spending time with family, traveling and putt-putt. I recently retired as managing editor of a small town Iowa newspaper. I am a former Marine Corps veteran, getting my start in the publishing business in 1981 working for several years on base newspapers. I spent time running my own freelance business. I love writing. I enjoy reading anything and everything. I also love the history of our country and enjoy reading western books, mysteries, and adventure novels, and watching mystery, adventure, and western movies.

www.ingramcontent.com/pod-product-compliance
Lightning Source LLC
Chambersburg PA
CBHW060304310726
48976CB00007B/2206